An Entirely New Country

Arthur Conan Doyle, Undershaw and the Resurrection of Sherlock Holmes (1897 - 1907)

Alistair Duncan

With a foreword by
Mark Gatiss

First edition published in 2011

Paperback ISBN 9781908218193
ePub ISBN 9781908218209
PDF ISBN 9781908218216

Published in the UK by MX Publishing
335 Princess Park Manor, Royal Drive, London, N11 3GX

This book is dedicated to my mother-in-law Isobel whose choice of gift one day made a good deal of this possible.

Praise for 'An Entirely New Country'

'It was evident from his first book *Eliminate the Impossible* that Alistair Duncan writes well, that he writes with knowledge and enthusiasm, and that he thinks about what he writes. His subsequent books, *Close to Holmes* and *The Norwood Author*, did more than just confirm that impression: they established him as an important commentator on Arthur Conan Doyle and his famous creation. After exploring the years when Conan Doyle lived in Norwood - surprisingly neglected by previous biographers, even though it was then that he became truly famous - Mr Duncan has turned his attention to the author's next decade, perhaps the most turbulent of his life. Undershaw, the house that Conan Doyle had built at Hindhead, was his home from 1897 to 1907. He wrote *The Hound of the Baskervilles*, *Sir Nigel*, *The Return of Sherlock Holmes* and much else at Undershaw. The house saw the end of his first marriage and the beginning of his second. He was resident here when he became Sir Arthur Conan Doyle. Yet, despite its cultural and architectural importance, Undershaw currently stands empty, vandalised and neglected. Read *An Entirely New Country* and you'll understand just why the Undershaw years were so important.'

Roger Johnson
Editor: The Sherlock Holmes Journal

'Alistair Duncan knows his Arthur Conan Doyle stuff. This excellent observation of the "Undershaw" period of Conan Doyle's life follows his previous fine appraisal of the "Norwood" period. Duncan covers the gamut of Conan Doyle's public and private life and comments fairly on what he sees as the noble and flawed aspects of his character.'

Bill Barnes
Captain (President) of The Sydney Passengers

'I have finished reading your book and have much enjoyed doing so. There is much that is new and interesting in it.'

Georgina Doyle
Author: Out of the Shadows - The Untold Story of Arthur Conan Doyle's First Family

By the same author

Eliminate the Impossible

Close to Holmes

The Norwood Author

Acknowledgements

Special mention is due to Mrs Georgina Doyle who was very generous with her time and permitted me to reproduce images from her collection of family photographs and extracts from the diaries of Innes Doyle.

Excerpts of A. Conan Doyle's correspondence from *Arthur Conan Doyle: A Life in Letters* co-edited by Jon Lellenberg, Daniel Stashower and Charles Foley (London: Harper Press, 2007) are used by permission from the volume's editors and the Conan Doyle Estate.

Others meriting thanks include: Bill Barnes, President of The Sydney Passengers; Lynn Beaugie; Patrick Casey; Carrie Chandler; Catherine Cooke; Phil Cornell; The Museum of Farnham; Rachel Foss, The British Library; The Francis Frith Collection; Lynn Gale, The Undershaw Preservation Trust; Mark Gatiss, Patron of The Undershaw Preservation Trust; Roger Johnson; Serena Jones; Michael Kilgarriff, The Irving Society; Jon Lellenberg; Brian Pugh; The Sherlock Holmes Society of London; Paul Spiring; Dr. Richard Sveum; Henry Zecher.

The photographs and other images used within this book have come from many collections including that of the author. None are to be used without the permission of the owner of the relevant collection.

About the author

Alistair Duncan has been a Sherlock Holmes enthusiast since 1982 and has spoken on radio, television and at live events about both Sherlock Holmes and his creator Sir Arthur Conan Doyle.

He is a member of The Sherlock Holmes Society of London, The Arthur Conan Doyle (Crowborough) Establishment and The Sydney Passengers.

He lives with his wife in South London.

'We accomplished our change very nicely, though Touie has had to acclimatize a little. The difference of 800 feet makes I am sure more change of climate in England than 4000 would do in Central Europe. You are living in an entirely new country to all intents.'[1]

[1] Excerpt from a letter written by Arthur Conan Doyle to his mother in October. *Arthur Conan Doyle: A Life in Letters* edited by Jon Lellenberg et al.

Contents

Foreword

A snapshot is a very revealing thing. Arthur Conan Doyle spent only a few short years at Undershaw, yet, in Alistair Duncan's fascinating and hugely readable book, much of his complex, sometimes contradictory, personality is illuminated. Here we see the homebody who was an active member of the local golf club, but also the patriot bravely volunteering for service in the Boer War. Here we see him as the dutiful husband, building a house especially to benefit his ailing wife, whilst simultaneously conducting a semi-scandalous relationship with a younger woman right under his wife's nose. And, of course, most excitingly we see the genius writer casually resurrecting Sherlock Holmes (for the money) and producing some of the very best stories in the canon.

Although the details of Doyle's diary have long been available, it's fascinating to see events set into the context of life at Undershaw. From the account of how 'The Dancing Men' may well have emerged from the editor's plea for a story with a juicy murder, to the memorable day that Doyle bowled out W.G. Grace, Duncan carefully and unsensationally documents a neglected period of the great man's life. It's an approach of which Holmes himself would have approved. For in the day-to-day, in the minutiae, much is revealed: the domestic arrangements of Doyle's butler which may have influenced the creation of the Barrymores from 'Hound of the Baskervilles'; the bizarre Sculptograph machine (and its unhappy sequel) invented by a man named Bontempi and from which 'The Six Napoleons' may have sprung; and the evidently friendly relations between Doyle and Bertram Fletcher-Robinson which should finally put to bed any conspiracy theories about authorship. I also loved the accounts of the reception given to the William Gillette play: “I…urge actors and actresses to make their voices heard distinctly. This duty, often neglected by stars to whom the public has been too indulgent, ought surely to be paramount with the acting profession”. *Plus ca change, plus ca la meme chose*, as Gustav Flaubert didn’t write to George Sand.

Many of the extraordinary talents and personalities of the time wander not only through these pages, but through Undershaw itself. This charming book stands not only as a testament to a crucial and hugely productive period in the life of one of our greatest storytellers but as a proud call to arms for his house’s preservation. After all, if Sherlock Holmes could so happily return from the dead, surely Undershaw can too?

Mark Gatiss, London, September 2011.

Introduction

When my last book, *The Norwood Author*, was published I thought I would finally, after three solid years of research and writing, take a rest from my Sherlockian / Doylean efforts. I even went so far as to say, in an interview, that I would confine any further such efforts to short articles for society journals.

As I have got older I have come to believe more and more in fate and, once again, that lady took matters out of my hands. *The Norwood Author* started to receive good reviews almost immediately from Sherlockians and non-Sherlockians alike and, perhaps inevitably, I started to get asked what I would be tackling next.

In reality I was giving some thought to writing fiction but did not wish to say so and thus create expectations. So instead I said that I had nothing planned at all.

This was not good enough for some of what I might tentatively term my admirers. Many of them took it upon themselves to find my idle hands something to do.

At the time the campaign to save Conan Doyle's former home in Surrey was making headlines and I had had some peripheral involvement with it. One of its principal organisers, Lynn Gale, was amongst those who dropped decidedly unsubtle (yet charming) hints that a book which revolved around Undershaw would be a good project. Yet, despite such suggestions, I resisted.

In May 2010, as part of the events surrounding The Sherlock Holmes Society of London's annual general meeting, my wife and I went for lunch at the Criterion Restaurant (a fitting place for the commencement of any Sherlockian or Doylean project). During the course of our delightful lunch the society president, Guy Marriot, indicated that there was certainly room for an Undershaw book.

It was then that I decided to bow to the pressure and take on the task. I hope that you find the result interesting.

Alistair Duncan, London 2011.

Before Undershaw

The nomadic years (December 1894 - October 1897)

Tuesday October 19th 1897[2] saw Arthur Conan Doyle and his family take up residence at their new Hindhead home - Undershaw. It was their first permanent home since December 1894 when they had left 12 Tennison Road in South Norwood. The intervening years had seen them live mainly in hotels in countries such as Switzerland and Egypt.

The decision to live in those countries was motivated entirely by Louise Conan Doyle's tuberculosis (or consumption as it was known). The aforementioned countries possessed climates that were understood to be beneficial for the condition so it was natural for Conan Doyle to take his wife wherever necessary to ensure her good health.

Such a nomadic existence was never viable as a long-term solution especially when it came to the disruption created for their children Mary and Kinglsey. Therefore Conan Doyle must have been pleased when a friend, and tuberculosis sufferer, named Grant Allen, informed him, in the first six months of 1895, that Hindhead in Surrey had a climate that was understood to be beneficial for those suffering from tuberculosis[3].

---

[2] From a letter sent by Conan Doyle to his mother on October 12th 1897 which stated that he was moving into Undershaw in a week's time.

[3] *Arthur Conan Doyle: A Life in Letters* edited by Jon Lellenberg et al.

Conan Doyle lost little time upon hearing this news and in July 1895 he wrote to his mother informing her that he had paid the deposit on the land upon which his new house would be built. The family were finally brought back to England in 1896 in order that Conan Doyle could more closely monitor the completion of his new house as well as attend to a number of UK based commitments. For the latter half of 1896 the family lived in Greyswood Beeches, a house in nearby Haslemere, before moving into the Moorlands Hotel in Hindhead in January 1897.

Despite the financial rewards that his writing had brought him it is clear that the cost of travel, accommodation and building was depleting Conan Doyle's bank balance at a rate that alarmed him. At the time he was busy working on *The Tragedy of the Korosko* which was due to begin serialisation in May 1897 but the state of his finances was such that in February he felt compelled to write to *The Strand*'s editor Herbert Greenhough Smith to ask for an advance.

The two men had previously agreed a deal whereby Conan Doyle would be paid £900 upon delivery of the completed manuscript. Due to the financial pressure he was under Conan Doyle sought some flexibility on Smith's part. In his letter he referred to his large builder's bill and asked Smith if it would be possible to let him have the £900 immediately. By way of encouragement to Smith he pointed out that the manuscript would be finished at the end of the coming week so he was not asking Smith to go out on too much of a limb. The letter's postscript indicated a level of urgency requesting a swift response concerning the matter[4].

Approximately eight thousand pounds later and over two years after buying the land the family were finally able to move in and life for them returned to something approaching normality[5].

---

[4] The letter is held at the British Library.

[5] The amount, according to Georgina Doyle, appears in Conan Doyle's account book. He quoted a sum two thousand pounds less to his

Herbert Greenhough Smith - Editor of The Strand Magazine

Conan Doyle's nomadic existence had, remarkably, failed to stem the tide of his literary output. The years prior to Undershaw saw the publication of many significant works including his semi-autobiographical work *The Stark Munro Letters* (1895), *Rodney Stone* (1896) and *Uncle Bernac* (1897).

---

mother in a letter (*Arthur Conan Doyle: A Life in Letters* edited by Jon Lellenberg et al.)

Now that he once again had a permanent base he was able to concentrate on his writing without having the added logistical and financial burdens of moving his family from country to country.

Once firmly settled back in England it appears that Conan Doyle lost little time in getting involved in local activities, the principal one of these being golf. Conan Doyle's love of the game had sprung up during his years living in South Norwood. His passion for it was such that it had led to him being demoted from the Norwood Cricket club's first eleven due to his apparent lack of practice and attendance[6].

Hindhead's golf club - The Hindhead and Hankley Common Golf Club - had been formed in December 1896[7]. Conan Doyle joined at some point during 1897 but it is not known precisely when. During his Norwood years, Conan Doyle had become a member of Beckenham Golf Club so it must have come as something of a disappointment to find that his new local club could only boast a nine-hole course. The drop in standard must have been a little frustrating. The desire for a superior course was shared by others in the community and when they eventually chose to act on this desire Conan Doyle was very much involved.

---

[6] *The Norwood Author* by your present author.

[7] *Hindhead's Turn Will Come* by Ralph Irwin-Brown.

Mary in the drive of Greyswood Beeches (1896)
(Courtesy of Mrs Georgina Doyle)

The architect's vision of Undershaw prior to work starting
(Courtesy of Mrs Georgina Doyle)

Moorlands Hotel in 1899
(Copyright the Francis Frith Collection)

Kinglsey and Mary outside Undershaw in 1897
(Courtesy of the Undershaw Preservation Trust)

1897

New surroundings

Once the Conan Doyle family were installed in Undershaw the house appears to have been deluged with visitors. One of the first of these (and the first name in the visitor book) was Conan Doyle's brother Innes Doyle who arrived on October 22nd - a mere three days after the family had taken possession. It is not too much of a leap to speculate that Innes paid for his stay by helping with the unpacking that was no doubt on-going at the time of his arrival.

The Undershaw visitor book
(Courtesy of Richard Sveum)

For most people the process of moving house is an arduous one requiring their full attention. Predictably, Conan Doyle seemed to be the exception. The day before Innes' arrival had seen Conan Doyle stir up public opinion by suggesting, in *The Times*, that Trafalgar Day (October 21st) no longer be overtly celebrated so as to avoid, amongst other things, upsetting the French. He proposed that Nelson's birthday (September 29th) be celebrated instead.

While this idea enjoyed support in some quarters, such as the *Aberdeen Weekly Journal*, it excited opposition in others. A man by the name of Arnold White, who wrote for the *Pall Mall Gazette*, objected strongly to the suggestion but appeared, at the same time, to be unclear as to where it had originated. In his attack on the idea, which appeared in the *Gazette*'s issue of November 4th, he suggested that the people behind the suggestion had 'not a drop of English blood in their veins' and were also no more than 'philosophic Semites'. A Jewish gentleman by the name of S. Schidrowitz evidently took some pleasure, in the following day's issue, in expressing much surprise at discovering, courtesy of Mr. White, that Conan Doyle was apparently both devoid of any English blood and was of Jewish descent.

Back at Undershaw, according to the visitor book, one of the first non-family members to see Conan Doyle's new house was his friend Henry Buchanan who arrived on November 9th.

Buchanan and Conan Doyle had first encountered one another when Conan Doyle had joined the Upper Norwood Literary and Scientific Society soon after his move to South Norwood in 1891. Buchanan was already society Secretary at the time and Conan Doyle had ascended to the position of society President by May 1892. When Conan Doyle left the area in 1894 Buchanan had supervised the election of his successor as president and had continued to serve as secretary until 1896[8].

It is not clear how long Buchanan stayed but given the distance between his home and Undershaw it would seem likely that he stayed at least a couple of days. Given the large number of people passing in and out of the doors of Undershaw at this time it is not likely to have been much longer.

In any event Buchanan's arrival must have been rather welcome to Conan Doyle. He had expressed a desire, in 1894 when he had stepped down as the UNLSS president, to be kept informed of the society's progress and Buchanan would have been able to fill him in on all that had occurred between his departure and Buchanan's own move to Staffordshire. Buchanan may also have been able to bring Conan Doyle up to date on at least some events in the Society for Psychical Research. Both men had joined the society, possibly with the encouragement of their mutual friend A.C.R. Williams, at the beginning of 1893 and Conan Doyle's almost continual movement since 1894 had probably made keeping up-to-date difficult.

On November 17th, Conan Doyle's brother-in-law E.W. Hornung came to stay along with his family. It seems reasonably clear, from events that followed, that Hornung sought his brother-in-law's advice about a legal matter and Conan Doyle suggested that he talk to A.C.R. Williams who was his friend and family solicitor. The reason for seeking this legal advice is not known.

November 26th saw what seems likely to have been the first appearance at Undershaw of Miss Jean Leckie[9].

---

[8] It seems likely that Buchanan stood down as Secretary of the UNLSS in May of 1896, when the society's annual general meeting was held, and moved (to Staffordshire) soon afterwards. We can infer the move from the fact that his name appears in the Croydon street directory of 1896 but not that of 1897.

Jean Leckie

---

[9] The Undershaw visitors' book was poorly used and despite being available for ten years only sixteen pages were ever filled. What is telling however is that Jean Leckie did not sign the book while Louise Conan Doyle was alive. Her first entry in the book occurs on August 5th 1907 a little over a month before she and Conan Doyle married and over a year after Louise Conan Doyle had died.

Jean and Conan Doyle had met for the first time earlier in the year[10]. Many sources agree that they had fallen in love almost instantly and this marked the beginning of a very awkward decade for them both. Conan Doyle found himself torn between the duty and love he owed to his ailing wife and the increasing passion he felt for the much younger Jean. He would spend more and more time with Jean over the coming years and be less and less guarded about his conduct. He managed to convince himself that he was acting with discretion and that his wife was very much in the dark about Jean's importance to him. Sadly, for all concerned, he was very much mistaken. Louise Conan Doyle was ill but she was not blind and her husband's interest in Jean was clear to her from very early on.[11]

Jean's first visit to Undershaw was for dinner and Louise's apparent calm speaks volumes about her self-restraint and respect for her husband - even under the most trying of circumstances. Her attitude throughout appears to have been one of realism and resignation. She had already lived much longer than had been believed possible and her concern appears to have been solely for the happiness of her children and her husband. Regrettably, although the latter was ultimately assured the former was not to be so.

On December 6th Jean visited again - on this occasion for tea. On this second visit she and Conan Doyle, accompanied by Innes and a Miss Halahan, walked to Waggoner's Wells, an area of Ludshott Common which consisted mainly of stream-fed, man-made ponds.[12]

---

[10] March 15th according to eight sources including *Arthur Conan Doyle: A Life in Letters* edited by Jon Lellenberg et al.

[11] *Out of the Shadows* by Georgina Doyle.

[12] According to the National Trust these may have been constructed for use in connection with the local iron industry in the seventeenth century.

Waggoner's Wells, Hindhead from around the period that Conan Doyle lived nearby
(Author's collection)

December 9th brought the first newspaper reports alluding to the existence of a Sherlock Holmes play although it seems, from the many articles that appeared over the following months, that it was not a big secret in theatrical circles. Conan Doyle had first raised the idea in a letter to his mother in September 1897 where he had stated that he was having serious thoughts about such a play.

The paper which carried the story, *The Northern Echo*, did not make a major issue of it. It was one item amongst many in their regular column *Jottings* and merited no more than a paragraph.

Beginning 'Sherlock Holmes is to be seen on the stage…' it went on to say that the play would feature many well known characters from the stories but that Conan Doyle had 'constructed a drama out of the series without embodying one of them.'

The article raised two questions. Firstly the origin of the information and, secondly, why it apparently appeared first in *The Northern Echo*. The paper was well regarded and was one of the principal newspapers of the north-east. Of potential significance was the fact that it would have been a newspaper available in Masongill, the community in North Yorkshire where Dr. Bryan Charles Waller, the man who had encouraged Conan Doyle to enter medicine, was local squire. More importantly it was also where Conan Doyle's mother Mary lived as a tenant on Waller's estate.

It is not unreasonable to speculate that the paper may have learned of this fledgling play either from Conan Doyle's mother directly or via someone to whom she had spoken about it. A letter written by Conan Doyle to his mother in December lends some weight to this theory. The exact date is unknown but its second paragraph begins 'All right about the Holmes play.'[13] This could be interpreted as a response from him to an apology from his mother about the article which he may not yet have seen.

Regardless of how it came to appear in print, the article could have easily been dismissed by all parties as idle speculation but soon other newspapers began to run more detailed articles. The first of these appeared in *The Glasgow Herald* of December 13th. The article was primarily concerned with the stage performance of Sir Henry Irving in Manchester the previous evening but it ended by naming Irving as one of the two men linked to the part of Holmes in Conan Doyle's play.

The other man linked to the part was Herbert Beerbohm Tree[14]. According to the article Tree had been the first choice

---

[13] *Arthur Conan Doyle: A Life in Letters* edited by Jon Lellenberg et al.

[14] Tree went on to found RADA (the Royal Academy of Dramatic Art).

of Conan Doyle but now the rumour was that Sir Henry Irving would, in the words of the article, 'be the original representation of Sherlock Holmes, a part hitherto attributed to Mr Beerbohm Tree.' The reporter behind the article did however acknowledge that any speculation was premature as the play was, 'hardly yet begun.'

Three days later the same paper ran a follow-up article. They informed their readers that, whoever played the part of Holmes, it would not be the great detective's debut on stage. Attention was drawn to the play *Under the Clock,* which had first been staged in 1893, where Holmes had been played by the actor Charles Brookfield. This follow-up article was most interesting in its closing sentence where the reporter stated that the new play 'will, I believe, not be altogether destitute of the love element.'

Speculation was clearly rife as to the nature of the play, who would play Holmes and when it would appear. The notion of the play featuring a 'love element' must also have excited some talk. A mere two days later the newspapers were once again running with the same story. *The Graphic* of December 18th attempted to clarify the situation. It began by stating 'Some confusion of ideas appears to be abroad regarding the play on which Dr. Conan Doyle is busily at work for Mr. Beerbohm Tree and HER MAJESTY'S THEATRE.' It went on to affirm that the play would be entirely original and that Tree would definitely be playing Holmes despite reports to the contrary.

Despite the best efforts of *The Graphic* the rumours around Irving continued. *The Belfast Newsletter* of December 20th reported the rumours in much the same fashion as the earlier newspapers but made no explicit mention of Tree's rumoured casting. Instead their reporter stated 'if it should prove to be something worth having there is a certain popular actor manager connected with a very beautiful theatre that would not mind reading the play to see if it suits him.'

Herbert Beerbohm Tree (c1910)

Henry Irving (1878)

This remark could easily have referred to Irving or Tree as both were actor-managers but in 1897 Tree had taken over as actor-manager of Her Majesty's Theatre upon which he had also spent a fortune in renovations. This therefore was more likely to be described as the 'very beautiful theatre' of the article.

In reality, most of the papers were inaccurate to some degree. The play, which was, according to the press 'hardly yet begun,' was in fact, according to Conan Doyle, finished during December[15]. When it came to casting there was no initial mention by Conan Doyle of involving Irving. In another undated letter to his mother, Conan Doyle mentioned that Beerbohm Tree was to have it for production.

However Conan Doyle was to become disillusioned with Tree. The actor, who apparently desired to play both Holmes and Professor Moriarty, requested a number of changes to make this possible. Presumably these changes mainly affected the scenes where the characters were due to appear together. Conan Doyle refused to change the play to accommodate Tree and withdrew it. He would later send it to Irving for his opinion.

December 17th brought the arrival at Undershaw of Sidney Paget. The famous Sherlock Holmes illustrator was now on a very different assignment. Instead of drawing the creation he was now to paint the creator. He did not commence work on the actual painting until the 20th so the days in-between were presumably spent on preparatory sketches and enjoying the hospitality of his host. Three days after this he was gone and there is nothing to indicate that he returned in connection with

---

[15] *Arthur Conan Doyle: A Life in Letters* edited by Jon Lellenberg et al.

the painting before it was finished. The short duration of his visit can probably be explained by the fact that his two children at the time, Leslie and Winifred, were only three and one years old respectively.[16]

Sidney Paget who illustrated the Sherlock Holmes stories in The Strand until his death

Boxing Day brought fresh guests to Undershaw. Amongst them was Conan Doyle's solicitor and friend Alfred Charles Redshawe Williams. Williams had been, like Henry Buchanan,

---

[16] Paget had six children at the time of his premature death in 1908.

a relatively close neighbour during Conan Doyle's residency in South Norwood as well as a fellow committee member of the Upper Norwood Literary and Scientific Society[17]. As with Buchanan before him, it was possibly the first time Williams had seen Conan Doyle since 1894 and he too would have been able to give his host details of activity in Norwood and the SPR[18] alongside the discussion on any legal matters. It is also highly likely that Conan Doyle mentioned to Williams his earlier conversation with Hornung and that his brother-in-law would be seeking Williams' legal advice.

As an aside it is tempting to speculate as to the state of the friendship between Williams and Buchanan. The latter's move to Staffordshire in 1896 would have forced the former to find alternative lodgings. The census of 1901 showed that Williams was living in a boarding house where he had presumably been since Buchanan's departure and the first we know of him living somewhere else was in 1904 when he signed himself into the Undershaw visitors' book as living in Tulse Hill.

Was it purely chance that the two men visited Undershaw on different occasions or was it the case that their host went out of his way to keep them apart?

---

[17] Williams had in fact been vice-president of the society and had lodged with Henry Buchanan prior to the latter's move to Staffordshire. More about Williams' earlier association with Conan Doyle can be read in *The Norwood Author* by your present author.

[18] Society for Psychical Research.

Arthur Conan Doyle as painted by Sidney Paget (1897)

Kinglsey riding Briggie in the drive of Undershaw in 1898
(Courtesy of Mrs Georgina Doyle)

1898

Disagreement, death and drama

January 1898 began with a disagreement between Conan Doyle, his mother and his sister Connie which concerned his solicitor and friend Alfred Charles Redshawe Williams. In the first known letter from Conan Doyle to his mother on the subject he was forced to mount a defence of his friend. From the content of the letter it seems clear that Connie was objecting either to Williams' service or fees and Conan Doyle's mother had taken up the cause on her behalf.

The curious aspect of the affair is that Conan Doyle disclaims any knowledge of the subject of the disagreement. As indicated previously, it would seem likely that Connie and her husband E.W. Hornung had sought Conan Doyle's opinion as to a solicitor, during their visit in November 1897, and he had directed them to his friend Williams. Conan Doyle probably also mentioned it to Williams when he, in turn, visited Undershaw on December 26th that same year.

Presumably, very soon after, the parties contacted each other with regards to their business and it was this that led to the disagreement. It is clear from his letter that Conan Doyle's faith in Williams never faltered and he gave examples of his friend's good conduct in order to convince his mother. There were certainly no long-term effects on the friendship between the two men as Williams would continue to be an occasional guest as well as legal advisor.

The Sherlock Holmes play received some further attention. Having withdrawn the play from Beerbohm Tree, Conan Doyle informed his mother that the play was now with Henry

Irving. It was clear that Conan Doyle was rapidly going off the whole idea. In part of the letter he stated his aversion to changing the story. He suggested that doing so would make Holmes different from the Holmes he had originally created and that he would rather just put the script back into his desk drawer and forget about it[19].

However it is clear that Conan Doyle did at least make the attempt to alter the play in light of the feedback he had received. An entry in his diary for February 10th makes clear that he was attempting alterations[20]. The earlier letter makes clear however that there was clearly a limit to the changes Conan Doyle was prepared to make.

March brought sad news in the form of the death of James Payn. Payn had been, in many respects, a literary mentor and had published Conan Doyle's historical story *The White Company* in the *Cornhill Magazine* (of which Payn was editor) in 1891. Payn's death had been expected as his health had been poor for some time but it still came as a blow to Conan Doyle. Such was Payn's popularity that newspapers up and down the land issued almost daily bulletins on the state of his health. Many of these reports appeared in the pages of *The Pall Mall Gazette*. The issue on March 17th drew its readership's attention to the fact that Payn had been suffering bronchitis for some five weeks. Their issue on the 23rd mentioned that the Duchess of Albany, the widowed daughter-in-law of Queen

[19] *Arthur Conan Doyle: A Life in Letters* edited by Jon Lellenberg et al.

[20] The entry in the diary is not too clear. 'Rewording Sherlock Holmes' could easily be 'Reworking Sherlock Holmes' but the implication is the same. While the entry does not explicitly state that it refers to the play it is the only Sherlock Holmes related item that Conan Doyle had on at the time.

Victoria, had sent a 'special messenger' to 'inquire as to Mr Payn's condition.'

The steady stream of reports ended on March 26th when the newspaper reported that Payn had died at five o'clock the previous afternoon. The article was decidedly odd in that it decided to applaud Payn and deride him in apparently equal measure.

After beginning by describing Payn as a 'prolific novelist' and a man 'equalled by few in popularity' it went on to state that it could 'not be pretended that he ever penned one single tale that will secure any appreciable fragment of immortality.' It was a decidedly odd and tactless way to refer to a supposedly loved writer[21].

James Payn (date unknown)

---

[21] In hindsight the assessment was largely accurate as little is said of Payn today.

The funeral took place on the morning of March 30th and Conan Doyle was one of the many who attended. Given his close association with Payn it is quite surprising that, according to reports, his part in the initial proceedings was minimal[22]. The coffin was conveyed from Payn's house, accompanied by four coaches containing family members and close friends, to nearby St. Saviour's church where most of the mourners, including Conan Doyle, were already assembled. Amongst the mourners were to be found a number of other famous names including the novelists H. Rider Haggard and Henry James.

After a service, described as being of 'the simplest character without choral accompaniment', the coffin was conveyed to nearby Paddington Cemetery by the original four coaches and, on foot, 'the friends more closely associated with the lamented author'. Conan Doyle was amongst these and was one of only four non-family members reported as standing at the graveside as the coffin was lowered.

At some point between the death and the beginning of April Conan Doyle must have been approached to write a small piece on Payn and this was duly published in the April 2nd issue of *The Illustrated London News*.

On April 4th Conan Doyle headed to Italy[23]. Accommodation for some of the trip would be found with his brother-in-law E.W. Hornung and sister Connie who were based in Rome. While there he had a dinner with Hornung and two other notable authors who were also in the area.

---

[22] *The Daily News* of March 31st 1898

[23] This is according to his diary for 1898.

The literary holiday (l-r) George Gissing, E.W. Hornung, Conan Doyle, H.G. Wells

The first of these, George Gissing, today relatively unknown, was arguably at the height of his fame at the time. From very troubled beginnings he had clawed his way up the literary ladder. He had, in his early days, been taken advantage of by his publishers who had regularly paid him flat fees for the copyrights to his work rather than pay him an on-going royalty. On the strength of this alone Conan Doyle is likely to have warmed to him given the similar experience that he had endured himself[24].

---

[24] Conan Doyle had been treated in a similar fashion by Ward, Lock & Co. when they had bought the copyright to *A Study in Scarlet* (1887).

Gissing was good friends with H.G. Wells who had, by this time, seen many of what would be regarded as his most enduring works published. *The Time Machine*, *The Island of Doctor Moreau*, *The Invisible Man* and *The War of the Worlds* were all available and the last had only completed its serialisation in *Pearson's Magazine* the previous year[25].

Curiously, with the exception of Hornung, the men all had complicated personal lives. Gissing had separated from his wife by whom he had two daughters and Wells, who had had numerous affairs, was now married to his second wife, a former student, for whom he had left his first wife.

After a few days in Rome, Conan Doyle headed back home via Gaiola, a small island off Naples, where he spent time with Nelson Foley - another brother-in-law[26]. He was back in England, according to his diary, by April 22nd.

On May 5th the *Daily News* reported that the first performance of the play *Medicine Man* had taken place the previous evening at the Lyceum Theatre. Amongst the notables listed as attending was Conan Doyle. Perhaps significantly it appears that he went unaccompanied as there was no mention of Louise or any other family members.

It is certainly possible that Conan Doyle was unaccompanied because the trip was as much business as pleasure. The occasion would have provided him with the perfect opportunity for a post-performance conversation with Henry Irving, the play's star, about the Sherlock Holmes play.

---

[25] Arthur Pearson, the magazine's founder, had been, until 1890, an assistant to George Newnes who apparently rated him highly.

[26] *Conan Doyle: The Man Who Created Sherlock Holmes* by Andrew Lycett.

Although it is not universally agreed, it appears that Irving had rejected the Holmes play. Whether he did this soon after receiving it or some time later is unclear[27].

The idea that Irving rejected the play was also supported, to a certain extent, by Irving's business manager, Bram Stoker. Stoker, most famous for his novel *Dracula*, wrote a biography of Irving which was published in 1906[28]. He stated that the years 1898-1899 were a difficult time for Irving. Irving had apparently been quite ill and was later to enter into negotiations with the Lyceum Theatre Company about selling his stake in the theatre. He would also have been quite busy with the play in which he was now starring. Under these conditions it is quite likely that Irving would have passed on the play. The only question mark, therefore, is over the date of the rejection[29].

Regardless of how Irving's direct connection to the play ended, the result was the same; the play had no takers and was available.

The man who was to breathe life back into the idea was American theatre impresario Charles Frohman who had arrived in England on March 24th, aboard the ship *St Louis*, with the aim of securing the theatrical rights to all manner of British works for performance in both Britain and the United States[30].

---

[27] Henry Zecher, in his book *William Gillette: America's Sherlock Holmes*, supports this rejection.

[28] *Personal Reminiscences of Henry Irving* published by William Heinemann.

[29] Also backing up the rejection theory is the fact that Irving was known to be averse to, what were then, contemporary plays. In 1888 he had handed the Lyceum Theatre over to Richard Mansfield for his production of *Dr Jekyll and Mr Hyde* rather than play the part himself. He was also later to pass on the dramatisation of Stoker's *Dracula*.

[30] The date of Frohman's arrival is recorded in passenger lists (source: Ancestry.co.uk).

William Gillette in 1895

One of Frohman's principal actors was William Gillette who had already built up quite a following on both sides of the Atlantic as a playwright as well as an actor. Gillette had been in England the previous year starring in his play *Secret Service*, which had been very successful in America and which was still playing at the Adelphi Theatre albeit with a new cast. According to press reports Gillette was in England again in February, very likely in connection with his play *Too Much Johnson* which was due to begin a run at the Garrick Theatre in April[31].

[31] We know Gillette was in England in February as *The Era* of February 19th reported him as attending a wedding in Marylebone on the 17th.

According to later reports, an American journalist working for 'an obscure newspaper, published in the Western States of America' had written an article which stated that Conan Doyle had voiced the opinion that the only man fit to dramatise Sherlock Holmes was Gillette. Conan Doyle had said nothing of the sort but the article found its way into the hands of Frohman who showed it to Gillette.

Charles Frohman (1856 - 1915) c1914

Gillette was amused by the article as, at that time, he actually considered the Holmes stories to be impossible to dramatise but suggested to Frohman that it would be a good idea to secure the dramatic rights[32].

[32] *Mr William Gillette as Sherlock Holmes* by Harold J. Shepstone (*The Strand* - December 1901)

According to *The Adventures of Conan Doyle* by Charles Higham, Conan Doyle's agent A.P. Watt had sent a copy of the play to Frohman after it had been withdrawn from Beerbohm Tree[33]. Mindful of his leading actor's advice on the subject, Frohman clearly decided that the idea should be looked into.

In March *The Era* of the 19th reported that Gillette and Frohman were amongst the audience at Wallack's Theatre in New York watching a play entitled *One Summer's Day*. It is certainly possible that the two men would have discussed Holmes and other works at this meeting before Frohman made his way to London.

Frohman duly arrived in England armed with his list of authors to contact. As already stated, he arrived on March 24th and conceivably could have met with Conan Doyle before the latter departed for Italy. However, given James Payn's death and the demands that the funeral and *Illustrated London News* article put on Conan Doyle's time, a meeting at this point seems unlikely. However, given Conan Doyle's return to England on April 22nd, Frohman could possibly have made contact in the closing days of the month and interested Conan Doyle to the extent that he would be willing to have discussions about the play with William Gillette.[34]

---

[33] Lycett disagrees and states that Conan Doyle bypassed Watt and used the services of one Addison Bright. Bright was a 'theatre specialist' that Conan Doyle had been brought into contact with by J.M. Barrie. The copy of the play that was sent was presumably the reworked one that Conan Doyle mentioned in his February diary entry.

[34] Conan Doyle wrote to his mother on March 31st (the day after Payn's funeral) that he was intending to depart for Italy shortly and spend three to four days in Rome before spending a similar period of time 'in the island'. *Arthur Conan Doyle: A Life in Letters* edited by Jon Lellenberg et al.

May 17th saw an attempt to lure Conan Doyle into politics. He noted in his diary for that day that he had received a visit from a Portsmouth Conservative deputation. At the time Portsmouth was a two-seat constituency with both seats being held by Liberals. At the previous election in 1895 the Conservatives had missed out on a seat by almost five hundred votes and the party clearly believed that a man like Conan Doyle, who was well known locally as well as nationally, would have no problem appealing to the electorate and taking one of the seats.

Conan Doyle did not answer immediately. He sent them on their way with a promise to give them an answer in a few days[35]. In the end he decided against the idea largely on the grounds that there was not, in his opinion, the prospect of an election for at least three years[36]. It was, in hindsight, a miscalculation as the general election that actually followed in 1900 saw both seats fall to the Conservatives. Had Conan Doyle's decision been different he could well have been in Parliament in 1900.

June 3rd saw Conan Doyle at the Hotel Cecil for the Anglo-American Dinner. The purpose of the dinner was to discuss, amongst other things, the advantages of an Anglo-American alliance. The precise nature of this alliance was not discussed so it is not clear whether this was a military alliance, trade alliance or an alliance of some other nature. For a man as pro-American as Conan Doyle, some of the press coverage following the dinner must have been a little depressing. The June 6th issue of Dublin-based newspaper *Freeman's Journal and Daily Commercial Advertiser* remarked on Conan Doyle's presence at the dinner and some of his speech. However they went on to remark that the 'function has, at any rate, had one

[35] From his diary entry for May 17th 1898.
[36] From his diary entry for May 19th 1898.

not unimportant result. It has evoked such expressions of opinion as show the hollowness of the suggestion about an Anglo-American "alliance"'. The paragraph concluded by saying of such an alliance 'the Americans don't want it, and England cannot get it'.

Hotel Cecil from the Victoria Embankment
(Author's Collection)

In July *The Strand* published a short story by Conan Doyle. It was entitled *The Man with the Watches* and told the story of a body found on a train with no ticket and no less than six watches[37]. The narrator of the story tells the reader of a solution which had been proposed by 'a well-known criminal

[37] Conan Doyle would later reuse the idea of a body missing a train ticket in his Sherlock Holmes story *The Bruce Partington Plans* which was published in 1912.

investigator'. Conan Doyle had completed the story on March 26th, the day after James Payn's death[38].

The difference between this investigator and Sherlock Holmes was that this detective's solution turned out to be incorrect. Was this Conan Doyle having a joke at his famous character's expense? His reluctance to name the detective may have stemmed from a deliberate desire to have some readers believe it to be Holmes but, at the same time, not to overtly harm Holmes's reputation while there was still the very real possibility of his Holmes play being put into production.

If this was indeed the idea it appeared to work. Certain elements of the press were firmly of the opinion that the detective featured in the story was *not* Sherlock Holmes. *The Bristol Mercury and Daily Post* of July 2nd mentioned the story stating, in their section *Magazines for July*, 'Dr Conan Doyle chips in with a new detective story, only, as Sherlock Holmes is dead, the mystery was not unravelled until the principal actor revealed the truth'.

Certain elements of the press, not content with getting themselves excited over this new mystery, then chose to get stirred up over a piece that had been published a month earlier.

In June Smith, Elder & Co. had published Conan Doyle's book of verse entitled *Songs of Action*. It was broadly well received although *The Daily News* of June 9th had stated that its best verse was *Song of the Bow* which was actually reprinted from *The White Company*, Conan Doyle's three-volume historical novel of 1891.

One of the new verses entitled *The Passing*, dealt with a man committing suicide at the behest of the spirit of his dead love. Some elements in the press found the piece morally objectionable as suicide was illegal and they considered the piece an endorsement of what was essentially a crime.

---

[38] Conan Doyle's diary for 1898. The work on this would also make it unlikely that he would have met with Charles Frohman before heading to Italy.

The Aberdeen Weekly Journal of July 20th reported on the presence of an article that had featured earlier in *The Star*. The article's author (identified only as 'J.D.') had leapt to Conan Doyle's defence by stating 'as I do not regard suicide as a crime (it may in certain circumstances be a duty), I cannot join in the outcry'. Going on to express sentiments that were certainly ahead of their time the article's author also stated 'our notions about suicide require revision.'[39]

The idea expressed in the verse of a death being the only thing standing between two lovers clearly had a parallel with Conan Doyle's own life albeit in a different configuration. It is tempting to wonder whether this parallel was something he was conscious of.

[39] This would not come to pass until 1961 when the Suicide Act passed into law making suicide legal but assisting it illegal.

A Problem Shared

At the end of July word started to resurface in the press about the Holmes play. In an undated letter to his mother, Conan Doyle stated that Charles Frohman had accepted the play. Although undated the letter also referred to the possibility (previously mentioned) of Conan Doyle standing for Parliament in Portsmouth. The letter makes clear that Conan Doyle had not quite decided about the Portsmouth seat although he was leaning towards not standing. This information allows us to place the letter, with some degree of certainty, on or before mid-May. So the agreement regarding the play had almost certainly been formalised between February and May[40].

The Era of July 23rd stated that 'Mr Conan Doyle and Mr Gillette are to collaborate in a drama entitled *Sherlock Holmes*, based on the best of Mr Doyle's detective stories.' It was further reported that Gillette had sailed for America two days previously and would make the play 'his next production in the United States.'[41]

On July 25th *The Era*'s report was backed up when *The Daily News* of that date reported that 'Dr. Conan Doyle has written a play on the subject of the adventures of his popular

[40] In the author's personal opinion a date in May seems most likely.

[41] A number of sources agree that Gillette and Conan Doyle did not meet in person until May 1899. Yet if Gillette was in England in 1898 at the very time that negotiations for the play were completed why did he not meet with Conan Doyle?

detective, Sherlock Holmes, in collaboration with Mr. Gillette, the author of "Secret Service."'

On the other side of the Atlantic, the August 11th issue of *The New York Times* carried a large article entitled *Charles Frohman's Plans*. As already stated, the article mentioned that Frohman had been in London for five months securing the rights to all manner of English plays for production both in England and the United States. It was the first report to completely lift the story of the Sherlock Holmes play out of the realms of mere rumour.

Under a sub-heading *Gillette as Sherlock Holmes*, Frohman was quoted as saying 'I have arranged for the return of William Gillette and Annie Russell to London, and for Mr. Gillette I have secured the dramatic rights for the world of "Sherlock Holmes", the dramatization to be made by the author Dr. A. Conan Doyle, and Mr. Gillette.'

Frohman went on to state in the article that it was Gillette's suitability for the role of Holmes that had persuaded Conan Doyle to sign over the theatrical rights which hitherto he had been disinclined to do[42].

At some point, after his return to the United States, Gillette got in contact with Conan Doyle over the changes he felt he would need to make to the play. It was during this exchange that Gillette asked if he might marry Holmes to which Conan Doyle famously responded 'You may marry or murder or do what you like with him!'

Conan Doyle had presumably been sufficiently impressed by Gillette and Frohman in order to relax his earlier objections to the alteration of Holmes. Alternatively it was possible that he was, to a certain extent, past caring and was focusing more on the likely financial rewards of the venture. The theatrical deal was subsequently reported, in less detail, in British

[42] Again, if the two men had not met by this time, it is difficult to determine exactly how Conan Doyle had been persuaded as to Gillette's suitability for the role of Holmes. Was it a decision based purely on Frohman's word?

newspapers such as *The Era* which mentioned it on October 22nd.

Returning to August, *The Strand* published another mystery by Conan Doyle. This was entitled *The Lost Special*. Once again a series of events was described by the narrator and, again, 'an amateur reasoner of some celebrity' offered a solution.

In this case the idea that it was Sherlock Holmes had a lot to commend it. In the detective's solution to the problem he states 'when the impossible has been eliminated the residuum, *however improbable*, must contain the truth'.

The overt similarity to Holmes's famous quote from *The Sign of Four,* right down to the italicisation of 'however improbable', made the identification of this detective as Holmes almost inevitable[43]. It is speculation but it is possible that when writing this story (late March or early April) the future of the Holmes play was less certain, in Conan Doyle's mind, than it had been earlier and therefore he was less concerned about Holmes's reputation. If this was indeed the case it might have been a little awkward for the story to be published right at the time when the project was finally gathering pace.

A curious article appeared in the September 5th issue of *The Bristol Mercury and Daily Post*. In their regular literary column *Our Library Table*, they provided a concise round-up of the month's periodicals. Curiously they described Conan

[43] The italicisation also appears in *The Sign of Four* (2nd edition) published by George Newnes in 1891 and *Round the Fire Stories* published by Smith Elder & Co in 1908 in which *The Lost Special* was reproduced.

Doyle's contribution to *The Strand* of that month as 'somewhat painful'. Such was their apparent discomfort with the story they neglected to mention its name or any description of the plot.

The story in question was *The Story of the Sealed Room* which Conan Doyle had finished on April 1st just before he had gone to Italy[44]. The story was macabre and owed a lot to Edgar Allan Poe in so far as it dealt with the discovery of a long dead body seated at a desk in the eponymous sealed room.

What is clear is that the management of *The Strand* liked the story as their adverts for the September issue gave the story top billing. In an advert that appeared in *The Pall Mall Gazette* the first line stated 'The Pioneer Holds his Own'. This could only have been a reference to Conan Doyle as a pioneer of mystery writing.

What is not clear is why *The Bristol Mercury and Daily Post* deemed the story 'painful'. Was this the emotion their reviewer felt upon reading it or was it a negative view of the story as a piece of work? In either event the decision to not name or describe the story was an odd one. The idea of death in a sealed room is one that Conan Doyle would ultimately revisit in his Sherlock Holmes adventures[45].

Amusingly, the *Daily News* of September 17th carried a long article which dwelt on the literature that they considered suitable for 'invalids'. Unsurprisingly the article considered anything by Poe as unsuitable but the article's author clearly had not read *The Story of the Sealed Room* as it stated 'The invalid may try almost anything of Mr. Conan Doyle's except his detective stories'.

The end of October saw yet another attempt to lure Conan Doyle into politics. In his diary for October 28th, Conan Doyle wrote that he had received a deputation from the Liberal Unionists who wished him to represent them. His main

---

[44] It would later appear in the volume *Round the Fire Stories* (1908).
[45] *The Retired Colourman* in *The Casebook of Sherlock Holmes*.

objection, according to the same entry, was the work load that it would entail. Amusingly the seat that he was being asked to contend was once again that in Portsmouth[46].

In their November 16th issue, *The Bristol Mercury and Daily Post* resumed their criticism of Conan Doyle. *The Strand* of that month had carried stories by both Conan Doyle and H.G. Wells. The former's was *The Story of the Club-Footed Grocer* and the latter's was *The Stolen Body*. Continuing their earlier practice, the paper elected not to name or detail either story but confined itself to saying of the authors that their stories showed 'neither of them at their best'.

Talk of the Sherlock Holmes play resumed in the media on November 24th. *The New York Times* of that date reported on a fire that had swept the Baldwin Hotel, in San Francisco, the previous night. In total the damage totalled one and a half million dollars and the report listed two dead, five injured and nine missing. Under the smaller heading of *Charles Frohman's Loss Heavy*, the report went on to say that property of Frohman's to the value of six thousand dollars had been lost in the fire and by far the most important of these losses had been 'the original manuscript of the dramatization of Conan Doyle's novel, "Sherlock Holmes," which Mr. Gillette has been working upon for the last three weeks.' It went on to state that 'it was the only copy of the dramatization in existence, and it will undoubtedly entail considerable time and expense to secure another copy.'

In fact the single copy of the play had been in the possession of Gillette's secretary who had been staying at the Baldwin. Gillette himself was staying at the nearby Palace Hotel. The secretary made his way to Gillette's hotel to inform

---

[46] *Conan Doyle: The Man Who Created Sherlock Holmes* by Andrew Lycett.

his employer of the loss. At 3 a.m. the secretary managed to rouse Gillette who, when told of the fire, is reported to have said 'Is this hotel on fire?' and, upon being told it was not, said 'Well, come and tell me all about it in the morning'.[47]

The Glasgow Herald of December 1st picked up the same story and reported the same loss. However they went on to state that 'The authors, of course, have their notes, but much of the dialogue, it is feared, is irretrievably destroyed, and must be rewritten.' Assuming the report to be accurate it implies that a good deal of the play, aside from its dialogue, was preserved in other documents.

The report concluded by stating that 'Mr Gillette will, after the New-Year, temporarily retire from the stage and re-write his share of the work, and the production of the piece will probably not take place till shortly before Easter.'

The Pall Mall Gazette of December 1st reported the plans for a dance on the 23rd to be hosted by Conan Doyle. Billed as a house-warming, the dance was to take place not at Undershaw but at the nearby Beacon Hotel[48]. The author of the report did not know the precise location and simply reported that the dance would take place 'at the Hindhead Hotel.'

The report went on to remark that the dance promised to 'be more than ordinarily interesting. All the guests will wear costumes representing the various characters in his books.' The reporter also remarked that the decision for fancy dress was not the idea of Conan Doyle himself but his guests as he was 'the most modest of men.' Leaving the subject of the dance the reporter went on to remark that Conan Doyle had recently been at a dinner in Southport which had been 'given by his

[47] *Mr William Gillette as Sherlock Holmes* by Harold J. Shepstone (*The Strand* - December 1901).
[48] *Out of the Shadows* by Georgina Doyle (chapter six).

admirers'. Be this as it may the reporter then went on to make a blunder by stating that 'Southport has close associations with the author of "Sherlock Holmes" for it was here that he established himself in practice as a medical man.' Of course it was in Southsea rather than Southport that Conan Doyle had established himself. It appears that no one thought it worth the trouble to correct the paper.

December 10th brought Conan Doyle back to the Hotel Cecil for the Christmas dinner of The New Vagabonds Club. *Lloyds Weekly Newspaper* of the following day covered the event under the title *Bishop and Vagabonds at Dinner.* Conan Doyle chaired the event and amongst the four hundred guests were the novelist Anthony Hope; Colonel James L. Taylor, president of The American Society in London and the Bishop of London Dr. Mandell Creighton. The bishop and his wife were the guests of honour and were seated to Conan Doyle's right at the top table[49].

After Conan Doyle toasted the Queen Anthony Hope got to his feet. Clearly as pro-American as Conan Doyle he offered the toast 'The United States and the Union of Hearts' which 'was accepted with much heartiness'. Hope went on to say how people devoted to literature found 'an open heart in America as well as an open door'. In response Colonel Taylor echoed the good state of Anglo-American relations and how the two countries worked best when they 'work together for liberty and progress as friends at peace'.

Conan Doyle rose once more at this point for the main purpose of the evening which, according to the newspaper, was to honour Dr. Creighton. The bishop was a prolific historical author whose major work at that time was a five volume work on the history of the papacy during the reformation. Conan Doyle regaled the guests with some anecdotes concerning the bishop's past and praised his contribution to historical literature.

---

[49] This is clear from an illustration that accompanied the article.

Mandell Creighton and Louise Creighton c1870

In response Dr. Creighton modestly affected not to recall the events of which Conan Doyle had spoken and in the spirit of reciprocation stated that he felt that the fiction published in the country today 'needed no apologies' and was 'generally in the direction of right'. After some further remarks on journalism, the event concluded with some songs performed by a Mr. William Nicholl who, apparently, performed with 'much charm of expression'.

The year concluded with an interesting piece in the newspaper *Freeman's Journal and Daily Commercial Advertiser*. In the December 16th issue, within their regular column *Literature,* they reported on Conan Doyle's election to Ireland's National Literary Society. Given his commitments it is clear that Conan Doyle was not present at his election.

Beacon Hotel, Hindhead 1899 (Copyright the Francis Frith Collection)

1899

Last minute concerns

1899 was to be the year of Sherlock Holmes' great theatrical triumph and the first words upon this subject in the press appeared in *The Era* of January 21st. In their regular column *American Amusements* they reported that William Gillette had resumed work on the play 'the first draft of which was destroyed in the Baldwin Hotel fire in San Francisco'.

Conan Doyle was soon to be engaged in a performance of his own. February 11th 1899 saw him give a public reading of his works at Toynbee Hall in East London. According to the newspaper reports he professed, modestly, to being surprised that anyone was interested in hearing him read.

Toynbee Hall c1900

The *Daily News* of February 13th described how Conan Doyle read from *Songs of Action*, *The Exploits of Brigadier Gerard* and *Rodney Stone*. Of Sherlock Holmes the reporter was only able to say that 'the distinguished detective was not so much as mentioned during the evening'.

The issue of *Lloyds Weekly Newspaper* that had come out the day before remarked that Conan Doyle had declined to give an encore and advised him 'not to forget "Sherlock Holmes" the next time he appears on the platform.'

What was the reason for this omission? Was it still the case that Conan Doyle's dislike of his most famous creation ruled his commercial head? If so he must have been encouraged by the fact that some young boys in his audience cheered when it came to his reading of the Gerard stories. It may well have occurred to him though, and possibly fuelled his resentment, that the cheers would have been louder, and not confined to the young boys, if he had read any of Holmes's adventures.

In one respect it was rather odd not to read from the Holmes stories. The forthcoming Gillette play had been mentioned considerably by this point and a fresh mention of Holmes in the media would have helped effectively advertise the play and stoke the demand for it to appear in Britain.

March 24th saw George Newnes publish a new magazine. Entitled *The Captain* it was, according to its own advertising, a magazine 'for boys and old boys'. The debut issue featured an article entitled *What I Wanted to Be*. This article featured contributions from, amongst others, W.S. Gilbert, Lord Roberts and Conan Doyle. Conan Doyle's entry was considered worthy of reproduction elsewhere and appeared, with one or two others, in *The Graphic* of April 8th.

'Mr. Conan Doyle told his master he wanted to be a civil engineer, to which that gentleman replied:

"You may be an engineer, Doyle, but from what I've seen of you I should think it very unlikely that you will be a civil one."'

April 7th brought a curious report in the pages of *The Northern Echo*. This newspaper, which had aired the earliest rumours of a Sherlock Holmes play, now published a short piece which suggested that their reporter was oblivious to known facts.

In its regular column *Jottings* the reporter stated:

'It is continually being asserted that somebody is preparing the adventures of Sherlock Holmes for the stage, and Mr William Gillette, the American actor and playwright, is now said to be tackling the subject in earnest. The truth is, however, that Dr. Conan Doyle has designs upon the character himself, and is not disposed to give up such rights of dramatisation...'

The article completely ignored the earlier press reports of Charles Frohman acquiring the dramatic rights and the earlier fire in San Francisco. Furthermore Gillette must have finished or nearly finished the new play by this time as he was soon to be in England for its first performance.

The Era of May 13th reported that a party containing Charles Frohman, William Gillette and noted American stage actor John Drew Jr. had sailed for England on the 10th by the steam ship *Paris* which had recently returned to civilian service after a short period as part of the U.S. Navy (where it was named *USS Yale*)[50]. The report also remarked that Gillette was 'collaborating with Dr. Conan Doyle in concocting a play out of the Sherlock Holmes incidents.'

[50] One of John Drew Jr's nephews was John Barrymore who would later play Sherlock Holmes on screen in *Sherlock Holmes* (1922). This film was based on William Gillette's stage play.

The SS Paris during its short service as the USS Yale (1898)

The ship arrived at Southampton on May 17th[51] and Gillette, Frohman and the rest of the party presumably made their way to London. Conan Doyle did not see Gillette immediately upon his arrival but, in a letter to his mother, he stated his hope of meeting the actor on May 30th and getting him to Undershaw for a weekend[52]. Despite his earlier telegram to Gillette, Conan Doyle was still uncertain about Holmes having romantic entanglements and desired to discuss the matter in person.

The story of their first meeting has almost passed into legend. Conan Doyle waited for Gillette to alight from his train and was left speechless when none other than Sherlock Holmes stepped down from the carriage. The figure walked up to Conan Doyle, studied him with a magnifying glass and then pronounced 'unquestionably an author'. The event amused Conan Doyle no end and proved to be an excellent ice-breaker. From this point on the two men were firm friends[53]. It seems reasonably clear that over the course of the weekend at Undershaw, Gillette laid Conan Doyle's concerns to rest as the romantic element of the play remained in place.

Conan Doyle clearly had high hopes for the success of the play and remarked, in his letter of May 29th, that he hoped that it would generate much income for the family[54].

---

[51] Ancestry.co.uk.

[52] Gillette did not sign the Undershaw visitors' book so we cannot be certain of the date of his visit.

[53] A version of this story is provided in Jack Tracy's *Sherlock Holmes: The Published Apocrypha*. However Tracy incorrectly states that the events took place in South Norwood.

[54] *Arthur Conan Doyle: A Life in Letters* edited by Jon Lellenberg et al.

The month of May also saw a war of words in the pages of the *Daily Chronicle* between Conan Doyle and the editor of *The Bookman* magazine, Dr. William Robertson Nicoll. It was considered so newsworthy that regional newspapers such as the *Leeds Mercury* of May 18th reproduced the exchange in convenient summarised accounts.

Nicoll had been responsible for a critical piece regarding Conan Doyle's recent matrimonial work *A Duet* and this had been published in both the British and American editions of the magazine. Conan Doyle had no problem with this but he did have an issue when Nicoll wrote further critiques anonymously in such journals as the *British Weekly* and *Sketch*. This, he felt, allowed one man to appear to be several and create the impression of a universal opinion of a book across the industry and with the reading public. He also expressed the opinion that, in some cases, the criticism 'may not be honest criticism, but may, consciously or not, be influenced by commercial considerations'.

Conan Doyle had undeniably raised some valid concerns but Dr Nicoll, in response, claimed that his various nom-de-plumes were well known or, as he put it, 'transparent' and 'interpreted to the reader'. When it came to the suggestion of the influence of 'commercial considerations' Dr Nicoll was incandescent saying that he was not sure that Conan Doyle should 'be answered more properly in a court of law than in a newspaper'.

Conan Doyle, perhaps realising that things had gone too far, wrote a follow up letter in which he accepted Dr Nicoll's assurances. He later wrote in his autobiography that he and Nicoll became good friends. Whether Nicoll saw things in quite the same way is uncertain as he died the year before *Memories and Adventures* was published.

Mr Holmes enters stage left

June 12th saw the first performance of *Sherlock Holmes* at The Duke of York's Theatre on St. Martin's Lane, London[55]. This performance was for copyright purposes only and was not intended as a formal event.

Conan Doyle stated, in a letter written to his brother Innes on June 17th, that the play was going to be 'grand'. He also remarked that he had discussed the play at length with Gillette and that his opinion of the play was very good.[56]

Given that this letter was written after the copyright performance, the suggestion is that Conan Doyle watched the play. Regardless of any conversations about the play between Gillette and himself at Undershaw, it seems reasonable to suggest that an actual performance would have been the best way for Gillette to demonstrate that his vision of Holmes was not something that should worry his creator. Seeing the performance would certainly have fitted into Conan Doyle's schedule as he was due to speak at a dinner that very evening being held at The Grand Hotel for the Anglo-African Writers'

---

[55] Frohman had taken over the management of the theatre in 1897 and was described on its literature as 'sole leasee and manager.' The theatre would later see the debut of *Peter Pan* in 1904 and would see Basil Rathbone tread its boards in the 1920s and 1930s. Rathbone, of course, later went on to become one of the most famous Holmes actors on film.

[56] *Arthur Conan Doyle: A Life in Letters* edited by Jon Lellenberg et al.

Club. The hotel and the theatre were only a few minutes walk apart so it would have been perfectly simple for him to have done both[57].

The New York Times of June 17th reported that Gillette had left London for New York the previous day. Curiously it described him as having remained 'long enough to see the single performance, for copyright purposes, of his and Dr. Conan Doyle's dramatization of "Sherlock Holmes"'.

If you choose to interpret the report literally, the implication is that Gillette did not play the role of Holmes and that he watched someone else in the role in order that he could watch the performance and see how it played to an audience. If this, perhaps unlikely, supposition is correct it would be interesting to know who took Gillette's part for this performance.

Despite the fact that there had been early press reports stating that the play would debut in the United States it seems clear that some elements of the press in Britain expected the play to debut in London. When it was finally determined that this was not the case the unhappiness was not overt. *The Newcastle Weekly Courant* of June 24th remarked:

> 'It seems that after all Dr. Conan Doyle and Mr. William Gillette's new play "Sherlock Holmes" is to be first seen in New York instead of London. Mr Gillette has arranged to produce it in November at the Garrick Theatre, New York with himself as the famous detective, and to bring it to London with the original company in the spring.'

Curiously the paper went on to remark that the 'the curtain falls upon a happy prospect of married happiness between him

---

[57] At the dinner Conan Doyle would counsel against rushing into war with South Africa. According to the report, in *The Northern Echo* of June 13th, he remarked that 'anything like the bullying of a small power by a large one was likely to cause irritation and was much to be deprecated'.

and Irene...' This demonstrated that the plot details were still very much under wraps and that this had led to the press making less than educated guesses as to how the play was structured and which characters it featured beyond the obvious principals.

Mid June also saw Conan Doyle hire his butler Thomas Rodney Cleeve. His diary for 1899 contained an entry for June 17th which laid out Cleeve's employment terms. He appears not to have made such an entry for any other member of his staff but perhaps he saw the management of the butler as very much his personal responsibility.

Cleeve's terms were rather interesting. His salary was set at forty pounds per year. On top of this was a beer money allowance of ten shillings a month. He was also eligible for a clothing allowance of one pound per quarter.

Thomas Cleeve was thirty-six years old at the time he entered Conan Doyle's employment. He was also a married man. His wife Elizabeth, to whom he had been married for four years, also entered Conan Doyle's employment as parlour maid[58]. The absence of a reference to her in the diary makes it difficult to determine whether or not she was hired at the same time as her husband or later. In any event her exact employment terms are unknown.

Two aspects of Cleeve's background would almost certainly have appealed to Conan Doyle. Firstly he had been born in Fratton near Portsmouth; secondly he had a military background having served as a Ward Room Servant on HMS Foxhound[59]. It was clearly this that had prepared him for his civilian role as a butler.

---

[58] 1901 Census.
[59] 1881 Census.

❧

The enduring popularity of Sherlock Holmes was demonstrated (if it really needed demonstrating) by *The Pall Mall Gazette*. In its issue of July 25th they ran an article on the literature that appealed to young people. The publishers of the 'boyish' *Captain* magazine asked readers between the ages of fourteen and twenty to give the names of their favourite characters in fiction. According to the article as the votes came in the contest became a two-horse race between Sherlock Holmes and D'Artagnan of *The Three Musketeers* fame.

The newspaper chose to focus on four opinions. Three of these were from boys and one was from 'a girl competitor'. The first boy expressed his preference for the musketeer acknowledging that 'It may seem an unpardonable offence in a British schoolboy to say that his favourite character in fiction is drawn from the work of a French novelist'.

The girl and boy that followed expressed a preference for character from Dickens and Thackeray respectively. It was the final contributor that spoke up for Holmes saying, in conclusion, 'I shall always consider that Dr. Conan Doyle has endowed the literary world - especially the juvenile contingent - with a most fascinating character, one worthy of contemplation.'

The *Western Mail* of the following day reported on a cricket match held at Trowbridge between MCC and Wiltshire[60]. The focus of the article was MCC's second innings which had begun the previous day. For Conan Doyle it was not exactly a glittering sporting occasion. Although listed as a member for the MCC it was noted that he was absent for the first innings (which had taken place on Monday 24th) and only scored six runs before being bowled on the 25th.

So why was he absent for the first day of the match? In the week before he wrote to his mother and mentioned that the

[60] MCC is short for Marylebone Cricket Club.

match was coming up and that he would be playing on Monday and Tuesday. He also commented that Trowbridge was a difficult place to get to but that he felt duty bound to go as it was the first county game the MCC had asked him to attend. Yet, on the 24th itself, he was still at Undershaw and writing to his brother. In his letter to Innes he remarked that his future plans rested on the performance of Sherlock Holmes which was due to debut in the United States in four months. He also wrote that he intended to start on his 'medieval' book next winter. The cricket match did not even merit a mention. Yet soon after writing this letter he must have travelled to Trowbridge in order to turn out for the MCC the next day. The fact that the match was not even mentioned in the letter to Innes suggests that Conan Doyle had subconsciously downgraded it to the point where it simply did not register. His subsequent poor performance tends to suggest that his mind was more on the play.

August brought Conan Doyle's cricket week in which he took part in one-day matches against Haslemere, Grayshott and various other local clubs. All this led up to a two day match against Cambridgeshire at Lords. On the first day (August 30th) Cambridgeshire opened the batting. The *Daily News* of August 31st reported the score mid-way through the MCC's first innings.

Conan Doyle was already the outstanding player of the match. He had taken no less than seven wickets for only sixty-one runs. The newspaper, with understatement, described his bowling as 'effective'.

On October 20th Conan Doyle gave a lecture in Bristol. The event, which had been announced in *The Bristol Mercury* of October 5th, was the Clifton Subscription Lectures which were held at the Victoria Rooms, Clifton. The lecture was entitled *Sidelights of History.*

The subject of the lecture was how he wrote authentic historical fiction by making use of the newspaper reports of the time. *The Bristol Mercury* of October 23rd reported that he quoted passages from both *Rodney Stone* and *Brigadier*

Gerard to illustrate his point apologising as he did so for quoting his own works. His excuse was that he knew his own works better than those of other authors and would be therefore less likely to misconstrue them. He also read from, what the newspaper reported to be, a portion of an unpublished work entitled *Box Fight with the Bristol Bustler* which, the article stated, 'created much hilarity'[61].

Victoria Rooms, Bristol c1870

October 23rd finally saw the first public performance of William Gillette's *Sherlock Holmes*. The performance took place at the Star Theatre in Buffalo New York. *The New York*

[61] The Bristol Bustler had first been mentioned in *How the King held the Brigadier* which had been published in *The Strand* in May 1895. This was one of the stories later collected as *The Exploits of Brigadier Gerard*. However the unpublished work referred to has to be *The Crime of the Brigadier* which was published in January 1900 in *The Strand*. It was later released as part of *The Adventures of Gerard* in 1903 where it was renamed *How the Brigadier Slew the Fox*.

Times of the following day was very positive in its review and remarked that 'the company was called before the curtain at the end of each act.' *The Era* of October 28th also mentioned the performance and remarked upon the various 'thrilling dramatic situations.'

The play then did a brief tour of theatres in Rochester, Syracuse, Scranton and Wilkes-Barre en route to New York's Garrick Theatre[62]. The build up given to this performance was significant. In *The New York Times*, Edward A. Dithmar wrote that Gillette's performance as Holmes (based on earlier performances) appeared to come 'as a matter of course' and that, as an actor, Gillette was 'unsurpassed today'. Dithmar concluded by stating that much was expected of the play.

A separate article in the same issue of the newspaper remarked that the play would commence at the Garrick on November 6th and that it had been favourably received in the various towns in which it had been performed en route. It concluded by remarking that 'Gillette's fitness for his new role is obvious.'

The first Garrick performance, which was reported on in *The New York Times* of November 7th, was an undoubted success. The opening line of the review stated that 'Sherlock Holmes's triumph on the stage will equal if not fairly surpass his triumph in the circulating libraries.'

At the close of the performance Gillette was, in the words of the reporter, 'compelled' to make a speech. In it he stated that all faults in the play should be attributed to the playwright. The reporter interpreted this as Gillette laying sole claim to the play's composition.

The reporter did however appear to have an ambivalent attitude towards Gillette's acting:

'As for the acting, Mr. Gillette looks his part and carries it in his accustomed nonchalant and pictorially effective way. As for his

[62] *Moulding the Image: William Gillette as Sherlock Holmes* by Andrew Malec.

expressions of desperate resolve, of heart-weariness, of sentimental love, they may serve or not, according to the imagination of the spectator. But much depends, always, on the actor's "vogue" and we fancy that Mr. Gillette is enjoying "vogue" just now.'

In other words Gillette's performance, like beauty, was very much in the eye of the beholder.

On the night of Gillette's American debut Conan Doyle chaired an Authors' Club dinner[63]. The guest of honour was Lord Wolseley. Wolseley was the outgoing commander-in-chief of the armed forces - a position he was about to surrender to Lord Roberts.

The second Boer War was almost a month old and this was naturally uppermost in the minds of many. Wolseley had no affection for the Boers referring to them as 'the most ignorant he had ever been brought into contact with'.

He went on to tell the assembled company that it was, in his opinion, the aim of the Boers to not only control the Transvaal but the whole of South Africa and that his fellow countrymen needed to remember this during the campaign. He naturally expressed his belief that Britain would ultimately triumph.

Despite the fact that he and Wolseley agreed on a number of issues it is fortunate that people like Conan Doyle had the ear of the nation at this time. The commendable even-handedness he would show throughout the campaign was a welcome and necessary counterweight to the opinions and attitudes of men like Wolseley.

[63] Source: *The Belfast Newsletter* of November 7th 1899.

Lord Wolseley.
Commander-in-chief of the armed forces between 1895 and 1900

❧

The period between *Sherlock Holmes*'s U.S. debut and the opening at the Garrick saw an unhappy event. Grant Allen, the man who suggested Hindhead to Conan Doyle as somewhere to live, died.

Allen was towards the end of his book *Hilda Wade: A Woman with Tenacity of Purpose* when he fell ill. When it was clear that recovery was unlikely, Allen spoke with Conan Doyle regarding how he proposed the final part should end and the latter wrote it up. It was later published under the fitting subtitle *The Episode of the Dead Man Who Spoke*. The publishers, in their notes, said the following:

> The last chapter of this volume had been roughly sketched by Mr. Allen before his final illness, and his anxiety, when debarred from work, to see it finished, was relieved by the considerate kindness of his friend and neighbour, Dr. Conan Doyle, who, hearing of his trouble, talked it over with him, gathered his ideas, and finally wrote it out for him in the form in which it now appears--a beautiful and pathetic act of friendship which it is a pleasure to record.

The *Glasgow Herald* of December 11th, in its music and theatre section, reported that Sir Henry Irving had suggested that Gillette's Sherlock Holmes play could open at the Lyceum the following spring. The newspaper went on to express the hope, even at this stage, that Irving himself would play the title role although they also acknowledged that it would be unlikely.

Given that they could not possibly have been in ignorance of the fact that the play was already being performed in the United States their desire to see Irving in the role rather then Gillette suggests either an impatience for the play to reach British shores or a desire to see someone other than Gillette play the role.

Grant Allen (date unknown)

In the closing part of the year Conan Doyle made his attempt to enlist for the war in South Africa. His attempt to do so both angered and scared his mother who was firmly against it. The press however made much of it and reports of his attempt to sign up made it into newspapers all over the country. The *Aberdeen Weekly Journal* of December 22nd mentioned that Conan Doyle had volunteered and would, if accepted, provide his own horse. The *Derby Mercury* of the 27th reported much the same commenting on Conan Doyle's 'hearty patriotism'. They informed their readers that when Conan Doyle was informed that the army reserves had been 'called out' his response had been:

> 'Reserves! We have not begun to touch our reserves. The reserves of this country are its hunting and shooting men, its sportsmen of all sorts, its cricketers and footballers. When we have come to these, I shall be sorry for any force that has to stand up against them. '

Only a few days before, on December 18th, he had also written to *The Times* to express his opposition to the idea, put forward, as he put it, 'from many quarters' that civilians drawn from the Empire should be sent to fight in South Africa. He stated that it was not right to expect civilians from the Empire to take up arms when those in Britain had yet been asked to do so. 'Great Britain is full of men who can ride and shoot' he went on to say and further remarked that the war had demonstrated that, it 'only needs a brave man and a modern rifle to make a soldier'. This last remark was a clear reference to the Boers although it is possible that some readers failed to pick up on it.

Kingsley turned seven in 1899
(Courtesy of Georgina Doyle)

Mary turned ten in the same year
(Courtesy of Georgina Doyle)

1900

Action at last

Conan Doyle was finally to get his longed for experience of war but as a medical officer rather than a soldier. This would have been an immense relief to his mother who had written to him at Christmas to remind him how many people were dependent on him and that he should not be risking his life. The only way Conan Doyle was able to placate her was to let her know about his new plans.

One of his friends by the name of John Langman had decided to fund a hospital for the care of injured and sick troops in the South African campaign. His son Archibald was to be the general manager (in some reports he was listed as treasurer) and he (Archibald) had already selected the head surgeon Robert O'Callaghan. The younger Langman approached Conan Doyle to help him select the remaining personnel and also invited him the join the staff[64].

Having made up his mind to go, Conan Doyle needed to make a will. He had assured his mother that the family would be financially secure in the event of his death but he realised he needed a will in order to ensure that, should the worst happen, things would go as smoothly as possible.

---

[64] John Langman would, in 1906, be awarded a Baronetcy for his services to the state. He became Sir John Langman, Baronet of Eaton Square in the City of Westminster. The title passed to his son Archibald in 1928. The short-lived title came to an end with the death of the third Baronet in 1985.

He clearly sat down and drafted his will in January as he wrote to his mother in the same month to let her know that he had left her four thousand pounds[65]. The fact that this was a draft seems clear thanks to a letter from February in which he informed her that he was soon to settle all legal matters with A.C.R. Williams.

The settling of the legal affairs was not simply confined to formalising the will. Conan Doyle had also decided that his trusted friend and solicitor should also have power of attorney[66]. This decision was probably not only motivated by the desire to have someone in this position that had legal knowledge but also because his brother Innes was in active service and could be killed in action. In order to ensure his family's security he needed someone who was out of harm's way.

According to the shipping records of *The Times*, Conan Doyle and his comrades set sail from the Royal Albert Docks on February 28th aboard *The Oriental*. The entry read as follows:

> Langman Hospital, Doctors, Conan Doyle, Langman, O'Callaghan, Gibbs, Scharlib, Howell, Major Drury, Dressers Hackney, Turle, Bolton, Blasson, Mayes, Civil surgeon Petchell.

The name of Turle is of particular interest. Edward Turle was the schoolmaster of Hindhead School where Conan Doyle's son Kingsley was a pupil. Clearly he was not the Turle on the shipping list but his brother Arthur Turle, who was four years older, was living in Oxfordshire and working, according to the later 1901 census, as a 'Surgeon General Practice'. The fact that Conan Doyle was involved with the fledgling hospital was no secret so it is perfectly possible that he and Edward Turle

---

[65] *Arthur Conan Doyle: A Life in Letters* edited by Jon Lellenberg et al.

[66] *Conan Doyle: The Man Who Created Sherlock Holmes* by Andrew Lycett.

discussed the matter and that the latter mentioned his brother as someone who might be interested in being involved.

Regrettably, further information on Turle, who went in the capacity of Dresser, is hard to come by and Conan Doyle did not see fit to mention the dressers in his autobiography. Consequently we cannot be certain that it was Edward Turle's brother[67].

A curious omission from the shipping list was that of Thomas Cleeve. Cleeve was, according to Conan Doyle's autobiography, taken by him to South Africa entirely at his own expense to assist as and when required. Cleeve's omission from the shipping list suggests that he was not deemed worthy of specific mention.

It may seem rather odd for a man to take an employee into a war zone and even more odd for an employee to go but Cleeve was suited to such a journey being an experienced sailor and military man. What Elizabeth Cleeve thought of her husband going to such a dangerous region is anyone's guess but she is unlikely to have been too pleased.

According to *The British Medical Journal* of January 13th 1900, Conan Doyle was attached to the Langman Hospital as 'Secretary and Registrar'. The former title simply meant that he was, in effect, the hospital supervisor. It must have been taxing in the extreme to juggle both roles. However, he rose to the challenge admirably, helping to calm down some potentially serious internal conflicts in the process.

According to *Memories and Adventures*, Conan Doyle arrived in Capetown on March 21st and stayed for a few days at the Mount Nelson Hotel which was relatively new. On the 26th he boarded ship once more and began the journey to East London, a city port on the south-east coast of the country.

---

[67] However he is the only Turle in the 1901 census that appears to be involved in medicine. This could, of course, be down to incomplete record keeping.

Upon arrival the hospital equipment was unloaded and the party made its way to Bloemfontein arriving, according to Conan Doyle, at 5am on April 2nd.

One man who, according to Conan Doyle, struggled from the first was Robert O'Callaghan, the senior medical officer. *The Graphic* of February 24th, in an article entitled *The Personnel of the Langman Hospital*, referred to O'Callaghan as 'a Specialist of repute in Abdominal Surgery'. The paper went on to say that his expertise would be particularly useful due to the prevalence of abdominal wounds amongst the soldiers. In practice, according to Conan Doyle, O'Callaghan was ill-fitted to the role for two reasons. The first of these was that he had led a very sedentary life and was therefore ill-equipped for the horrors and physical demands of a military hospital. The second reason was that he was actually a gynaecologist, a role which Conan Doyle stated, with characteristic wit and understatement, was a 'branch of the profession for which there seemed to be no immediate demand.'[68]

Also according to Conan Doyle, O'Callaghan soon came to appreciate his lack of suitability and left the hospital (and South Africa) not long afterwards. Conan Doyle was kind enough about O'Callaghan in his autobiography but he was less so in private. In a letter to his mother dated April 20th he mentioned that O'Callaghan was to leave the hospital and that he was very glad to be seeing the back of the head surgeon who he viewed as both fat and unfit[69].

However, Conan Doyle's low assessment of O'Callaghan cannot be allowed to pass entirely unchallenged. The unfortunate surgeon died only a few years later on January 10th 1903. Born in 1858 he was forty-five and thus only a year older than Conan Doyle. His obituary, which appeared in *The British Medical Journal* of January 17th 1903, described him as having an 'apparently robust constitution'. It did however go on to say

---

[68] *Memories and Adventures* by Arthur Conan Doyle.
[69] *Arthur Conan Doyle: A Life in Letters* edited by Jon Lellenberg et al.

that his death was due to cardiac failure. If he had been as fat and unfit as Conan Doyle had suggested his chances of cardiac complications were probably higher than average[70].

In this then Conan Doyle could be seen as being at least partly accurate. His assessment of O'Callaghan's medical qualifications and suitability for army medical service were, however, distinctly wide of the mark. O'Callaghan had become attached to the 1st Flintshire Royal Engineers not long after qualifying as a surgeon through the Royal College of Surgeons in Ireland. At the time of his death he held the rank of Surgeon-Lieutenant-Colonel which he would hardly have achieved had he been so ill-suited to the rigours of army service.

His qualifications were not in any doubt either. According to his obituary he had indeed studied abdominal surgery and had submitted papers on the subject to *The British Medical Journal*. Although he had worked briefly as a gynaecologist, at the Chelsea Hospital for Women, his career in that field only really began in earnest after the South African campaign. When dealing specifically with his time at the Langman Hospital, the obituary detailed that his efforts there had led to him being mentioned in dispatches and that he had received 'the medal and clasps'. Significantly, the obituary also suggested that he served at the Langman Hospital for some time.

So did O'Callaghan leave the Langman abruptly or did he not? Backing up the idea that he remained in service with the hospital was *The London Gazette*. The newspaper still listed him as the senior medical officer of the Langman in its issue of April 16th 1901 almost one whole year after the hospital staff arrived in South Africa and almost as long after Conan Doyle claimed O'Callaghan was leaving.

---

[70] However, a photograph taken of the Langman staff (before their departure) shows O'Callaghan to be of a similar build to Conan Doyle. He certainly does not look like the unfit and fat man that he was made out to be (Source: *Arthur Conan Doyle: A Life in Letters* edited by Jon Lellenberg et al).

This fact did not escape Conan Doyle's notice. In a later letter to his mother he remarked on the *Gazette*'s mention of O'Callaghan's work at the hospital and suggested to her, rather sarcastically, that they would be soon be reading of O'Callaghan's knighthood[71].

Bloemfontein, South Africa c1900

So how do we reconcile these two opposing views? Conan Doyle was physically there so this must give his version of events some weight. However, would the *British Medical Journal* and *London Gazette* both have made such errors with regards to O'Callaghan's army medical service?

A perfectly possible scenario is that O'Callaghan did indeed leave the hospital but that he later resumed work there after Conan Doyle had returned to England. After all, Conan Doyle's eventual departure from the hospital would leave a vacancy which John and Archie Langman would have been eager to fill.

Regardless of what happened, it reflects a little poorly on Conan Doyle that he chose to speak so disparagingly about

---

[71] *Arthur Conan Doyle: A Life in Letters* edited by Jon Lellenberg et al.

O'Callaghan. The two men may well have failed to get on but that was no reason to talk down O'Callaghan's medical prowess when there was much evidence that he was perfectly capable. Had O'Callaghan still been alive at the time Conan Doyle published his autobiography it seems possible that his passages on their time at the Langman Hospital would have been challenged.

The Langman Hospital commandeered the premises of The Ramblers Club of Bloemfontein and reports appeared in the press to that effect. *The Derby Mercury* of April 11th reported the takeover and stated that fifty beds for 'sick cases' had been opened in the building's gymnasium and that the operating theatre and tents for 'surgical cases' had been set up in the building's adjoining 'playground' (which Conan Doyle later referred to as a cricket field).

A few days after the hospital opened it was visited by Field Marshall Roberts who had come specifically to inspect it. In a later telegram to John Langman, which was reported in *The Graphic* of April 28th, Roberts stated that the Langman Hospital's 'value to our R.A.M.C. and wounded cannot be overestimated'[72]

Around the same time an artist by the name of Mortimer Menpes (1855 - 1938) visited to draw a scene for *The Illustrated London News*. Menpes recalled later that, although clearly overworked, Conan Doyle did not appear to lack energy[73]. The newspaper also sent a photographer by the name of Owen Scott. Scott took photographs of Conan Doyle with the Langman's patients. One of these pictures was subsequently used as the basis for an illustration by artist Allan Stewart. The resultant drawing gave a very reader friendly view of the Langman and did not convey anything of the real misery that was dealt with every day.

---

[72] RAMC stood for Royal Army Medical Corps.

[73] *Arthur Conan Doyle: A Life in Letters* edited by Jon Lellenberg et al.

The Harbour on Buffalo River, East London, South Africa 1899. The Langman Hospital equipment was probably unloaded here. (Author's collection)

Conan Doyle in South African 'uniform'
(Author's collection)

Field Marshal Frederick Sleigh Roberts, 1st Earl Roberts (1832 - 1914)

Mortimer Menpes' illustration of Conan Doyle writing. The similarity to the photograph below suggests that Menpes may have been drawing Conan Doyle at the same time as the photograph was taken..

In his autobiography, however, Conan Doyle made no secret of the punishing clinical workload at the hospital. He also made it clear that the full extent of the horror was consciously kept from the public at the time. The hospital was equipped to cope with fifty patients but at one point had one hundred and twenty which placed an intolerable burden on resources, staff and hygiene standards. Conan Doyle and his colleagues were rushed off their feet and on top of all this he had his role of hospital secretary. With all this pressure it is surprising that he managed to find any time to write. Yet find the time he did with *The Strand* being the natural beneficiary of some of his output. One such article, entitled *A Glimpse of the Army*, ultimately appeared in the magazine's September issue.

In the early part of June Conan Doyle wrote a lengthy article on life at the Langman Hospital for *The British Medical Journal*. In it Conan Doyle briefly referred to Robert O'Callaghan - although not by name. He stated that one member of the medical staff had left soon after arriving and that the position of senior surgeon had then been held by Gibbs. Whether this was an official appointment or not is open to question but it seems doubtful as Gibbs does not seem to have been listed as the senior surgeon in any official reports. At best it was probably an acting appointment.

Towards the end of June something happened that caused Conan Doyle to decide to return to England. He made no mention of what this was but if it was indeed the case that Robert O'Callaghan returned to the hospital (as the previously mentioned newspaper and journal articles suggest) news of his imminent return may have encouraged Conan Doyle to leave. It is speculation of course but it is certainly possible and would account, to a certain extent, for the later reports that continued to link O'Callaghan with the Langman. Alternatively Conan Doyle may simply have felt that he had done his duty.

Before he left, Conan Doyle decided that he wanted to visit some other parts of South Africa. On June 22nd he boarded a train to Pretoria but was back at the Langman by July 4th. During the trip he had a meeting with Lord Roberts which concerned the unsatisfactory state of military hospitals in the region. This was a subject already causing arguments back in Britain.

By July 11th Conan Doyle was back in Capetown (having left the Langman the day after his return from Pretoria) and boarding the steam ship *Briton* for the journey back to England. Amongst his fellow passengers on this journey was a *Daily Express* journalist by the name of Bertram Fletcher Robinson who was destined to have a significant effect on his literary output.

Conan Doyle writing at the Langman Hospital in Bloemfontein which appeared in the September 1900 issue of The Strand (Author's collection)

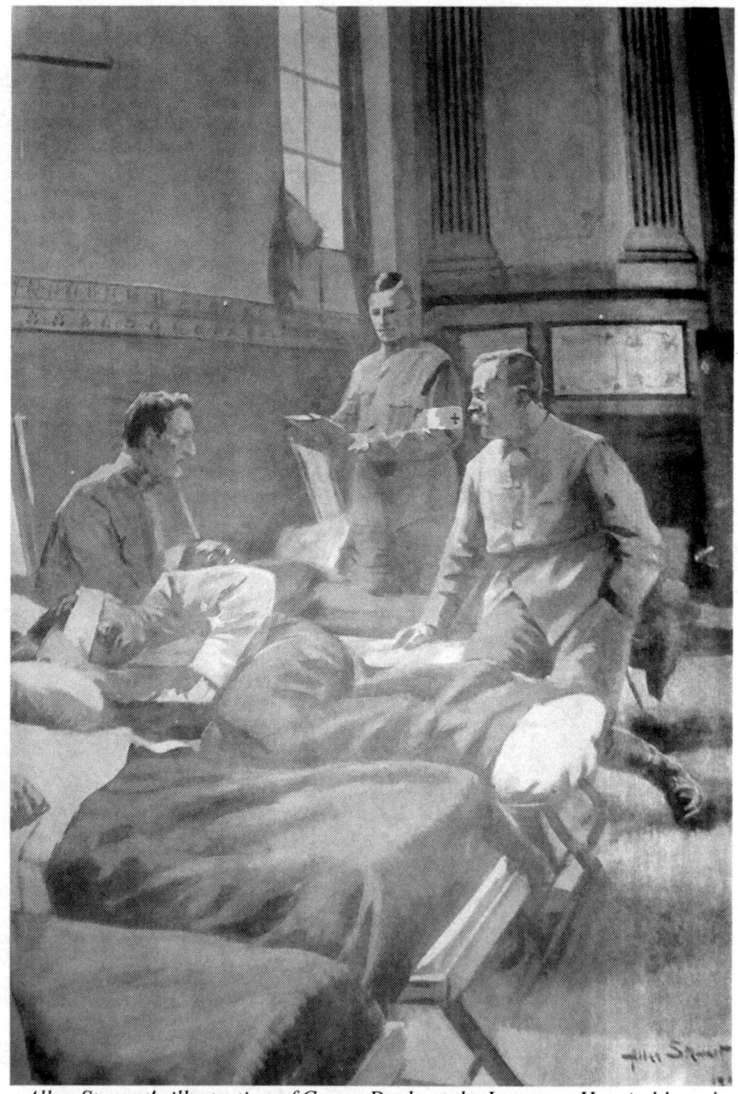

Allan Stewart's illustration of Conan Doyle at the Langman Hospital based on a photograph by Owen Scott
(Author's collection)

The Staff of the Langman Hospital (Conan Doyle is standing second from left) in 1900 (from Memories and Adventures)

S.S. Briton docked at Cape Town (c.1905)

Conflict at home

There had been much coverage in the media concerning the state of the military hospitals in South Africa. Mr William Burdett-Coutts, the Member of Parliament for Westminster, had raised questions over the quality of the care afforded and had made accusations against the government for their handling of the situation. Some of his examples of sub-standard care had concerned Bloemfontein which naturally brought Conan Doyle into the picture. Burdett-Coutts, it is important to note, made no direct accusations against any individuals in the field but confined his criticisms to the state of the hospitals and thus the quality of care that could reasonably be expected.

This negative opinion was by no means lacking support, with noted physician Sir Walter Foster and M.P. Sir Charles Dilke supporting Burdett-Coutts' position. The government, largely represented by George Wyndham, the Under-Secretary of State for War, needed supporters of its own.

The *Daily Express* of June 30th had detailed some of the events in Parliament and managed to interview Mortimer Menpes, the artist who had drawn Conan Doyle almost two months earlier.

Under the subheading *Dr. Conan Doyle's View*, Menpes described the accusations of Burdett-Coutts as 'Hopelessly exaggerated' and further stated, with respect to Conan Doyle, that:

'Dr. Conan Doyle worked like a horse, until he had to drag himself up on to a kopje to get fresh air, saturated as he was with enteric. He is one of the men that makes England great.'

He concluded thus:

'What amazed me was the cleanliness of the different camps and hospitals. I saw the putrid camps, just as Mr. Burdett-Coutts saw them, but I waited for a little, and I saw them clean and healthy.

'I can't do better than quote Conan Doyle: "I have quitted a novelist's life for the time being for that of a doctor in the field, and I am only thankful that as a doctor I have to work under such circumstances as I am at present"'.

Sir Charles Dilke (1843 - 1911)

Unsurprisingly the word of Menpes to a newspaper was insufficient and, soon after his return to England, Conan Doyle was called on to give evidence to an enquiry on the military hospitals in South Africa. According to *The British Medical Journal* of July 28th, the enquiry began on July 24th at Burlington House in Piccadilly. Conan Doyle himself was not called to give evidence until the 30th[74].

Burlington House in 1874

In response to questioning he reported that although he had seen overcrowding and knew that most hospitals were operating beyond capacity he had seen no evidence of neglect. The chairman asked Conan Doyle to confirm that there was nothing else he wished to report. In response Conan Doyle stated:

'I once had occasion to write to General Wilson and he received my suggestion. He put the matter right and thanked me instead of taking umbrage. I believe if men instead of taking criticisms at large

[74] *The Times* July 31st 1900.

had gone to the responsible head of department and pointed out what was wrong it would have been put right.'

After facing the horrors of the Langman Hospital and the enquiry the last thing Conan Doyle probably needed was aggravation. However aggravation was what he received. Not long after the enquiry he had a falling out with his sister Connie and brother-in-law Willie Hornung. The subject of their quarrel was Jean Leckie.

Conan Doyle was naturally keen to see Jean upon his return but made the tactless mistake of taking her to a cricket match at Lords as his guest. This was too much for Hornung and Connie who saw it as morally inappropriate and a slap in the face to Louise. Hornung remonstrated with Conan Doyle with the latter totally failing to appreciate how things looked nor that he had done anything wrong. He simply could not (or would not) see that flaunting a relationship with Jean, platonic or not, simply was not on. In his desperation he turned to his only real ally - his mother. She offered to intercede on his behalf but Conan Doyle refused. It would appear that his letter to her was more of a means to vent his frustration than a cry for help. There is certainly not much evidence that he altered his conduct in any way.

Conan Doyle continued his cricketing commitments in August. Between the 23rd and 25th a match was held between the MCC and London County at their home ground in the grounds of the Crystal Palace. This period was arguably the high point in his cricketing life as he not only obtained his first and only first-class wicket but it was the wicket of no less than cricketing legend W.G. Grace.

Grace had moved to the area in 1898 and had begun to play for the Crystal Palace team in the palace's park that same year. He was arguably at the end of his career and may have seen an opportunity for one last great success with the struggling team.

In 1899 he founded the London County Cricket Club and in 1900 they began to play first-class cricket[75].

Conan Doyle's memorable day took place on August 25th when Grace resumed his second innings from the previous day. This, in partnership with a Mr. J. Gilman, had resulted in his gaining over a century which was only the second time he had achieved such a score that season[76]. This impressive run was interrupted by Conan Doyle who caused Grace to knock the ball onto his own wicket. As if the heavens themselves disapproved, this was closely followed by heavy rain which caused an early lunch[77].

Following lunch, and an inspection of the pitch, Grace's side declared. Conan Doyle, when his turn came to bat, was presumably still too stunned at the famous wicket he had taken as he was bowled out with only four runs to his name.

It is not unreasonable to suppose that Conan Doyle would have stayed in the local area during these few days rather than commute from a central London Hotel. The area around the Crystal Palace was one with which he was very familiar from the days of his South Norwood residency. Conan Doyle seems to have made frequent use of hotels rather than impose upon family or friends but in this case it is doubtful that there would have been anyone to impose upon had he even been so inclined. As we have already seen, two of his closest friends from those years, A.C.R. Williams and H.B.M. Buchanan, had gone their separate ways. The former was now in lodgings in nearby Streatham and the latter was in Staffordshire.

Due to the number of visitors that the palace drew to the area there were a number of large hotels in the immediate vicinity of the park. There was however, at a slightly further distance, the Anerley Arms Hotel. The proprietor of this establishment had always made plain, in adverts that Conan

---

[75] *Ideal Homes: Suburbia in Focus (http://www.ideal-homes.org.uk)*

[76] *The Times* of August 27th 1900.

[77] Conan Doyle wrote to tell his mother about his famous 'scalp' two days later.

Doyle would have read in *The Norwood News* during his earlier residency, that he catered especially for sporting clubs and individuals. It is therefore not unreasonable to speculate that Conan Doyle may have spent some time at this hotel[78].

Dr. W.G. Grace c1900

What is clear is that his appearance at this match went unreported in the local press. This may seem odd but is consistent with the negative effect that the Crystal Palace had on all other attractions in the area. As soon as it had been relocated to the area from Hyde Park it had drawn visitors away

[78] If he did it might explain his decision to feature the hotel in his Sherlock Holmes story *The Norwood Builder* in 1903.

from earlier distractions. Many other attractions failed as a result and the palace's negative effect eventually also worked its spell on Grace's cricket club which ceased playing first-class cricket in 1904 and disbanded entirely by 1909.

❧

Meanwhile the press was still very much occupied with the events of the Boer War and, very much like today, spent a lot of time dissecting what it saw as the lessons to be learned by the army. This was a subject about which Conan Doyle was already dealing with in his book on the war but he had no objection to voicing his observations ahead of publication.

The Penny Illustrated Paper and Illustrated Times of September 8th referred to Conan Doyle's article in *The Strand* that had appeared only shortly before. After describing him as the 'popular novelist and bright, cheery Briton, patriotic to the core' they went on to tell how Conan Doyle had noted that the army's officers were too inclined to nag. They quoted Conan Doyle as saying:

> 'They halt for a midday rest, and it seems to me, as I move among them, that there is too much nagging on the part of the officers. We have paid too much attention to German military methods.'

Conan Doyle's opinion was that the British army would do better in future if it were to model itself after that of the United States. He went on to complain about the conduct of a 'Colonial corps of cavalry' which he would not name and how they had failed to employ scouts and other, what he saw as, basic elements of military best practice. He stated that the British army needed to find an equivalent to Napoleon and concluded by saying that 'only a man with such powers can ever thoroughly reorganise our Army'.

He now turned his attention to the completion of his book and by October Smith Elder & Co. published *The Great Boer War*. Conan Doyle dedicated it to John Langman as follows:

John L. Langman
Who devoted his fortune, and that which was more valuable to him than his fortune, to the service of his country and to the relief of suffering.[79]

Conan Doyle was not a man to pull his punches and he knew his book was likely to cause a stir. He wrote to his mother about it and stated that he expected a 'storm' to break at some point[80].

In the meantime he was diverted by the general election. *The Times* of September 25th had reported that he had been adopted unanimously as the Liberal Unionist candidate for the seat of Edinburgh Central. Almost a month earlier his election agent had suggested that he fight Dundee and Conan Doyle had declined, stating later to his mother that he considered the city an 'odious' place.[81]

The Edinburgh seat was very much a safe one for the Liberal Party and the Liberal Unionists faced an uphill battle if they were to take it. The sitting M.P. was William McEwan who had held the seat since 1886. McEwan had decided to retire so Conan Doyle was fighting against the new Liberal candidate George Mackenzie Brown.

In a letter dated August 31st 1900, and almost certainly written by the party secretary John Boraston, the Liberal Unionist Association had briefed Conan Doyle that Brown was not a credible threat. They pointed out that he was not known in

---

[79] The more valuable something that Conan Doyle alluded to was probably John Langman's son Archie.

[80] *Arthur Conan Doyle: A Life in Letters* edited by Jon Lellenberg et al.

[81] As above.

the city and was considered by all to be an 'untried man'. They also stated that an informant who knew Brown was of the firm opinion that he would not 'catch on' or create any enthusiasm. The letter concluded by expressing the belief that it was the opinion on the ground that the largely working class constituency would go 'nearly solid' for Conan Doyle, if he were to stand[82].

Brown was indeed a political unknown and was the head of Thomas Nelson and Sons, a prominent Edinburgh based publisher. However Brown was not entirely without political experience. His father, George Brown, had been leader of the Liberal Party of Canada West so it is reasonable to assume that he had some idea of what he was involving himself in. The awkward aspect was that Thomas Nelson and Sons published some of Conan Doyle's work. However this clearly had no long-term effect on their relationship as the company would continue to publish Conan Doyle's works long after the election[83].

On September 24th Conan Doyle had written to *The Edinburgh Evening Dispatch.* His letter was a direct appeal to the voters in the constituency. He suggested that they should cast their vote based almost entirely on the one issue of the Boer War. He implied that it was in their best interests to keep the government in power as it would ensure that the war was conducted in Britain's best interests.

---

[82] Letter held at the British Library. The end of the letter is missing which is why the name of the author is not known for certain.

[83] The company later published the second English edition of *The Great Boer War.* Conan Doyle objected to the first impression they produced on several grounds. Most notable amongst the reasons was the decision to put Sir Arthur Conan Doyle on the spine rather than A. Conan Doyle which he preferred. The second notable reason was that they included a full page photograph of Conan Doyle on the frontispiece. Conan Doyle refused to sanction the issue and it was destroyed. A new issue replacing his image with that of Lord Roberts and correcting the other faults was published a short while later. (Source: *A Bibliography of A. Conan Doyle* by Gibson and Green).

His highly visible campaign stirred up some opposition and it was suggested by some that it was improper for a member of the Reform Club - which was very much a bastion for the Liberal Party - to be advocating the merits of the Conservative government. The criticism stung Conan Doyle who wrote to *The Daily Chronicle* to defend himself and state that he would submit to the club committee's judgment on the issue.

The Penny Illustrated Paper and Illustrated Times of October 6th ran an article on the election. In addition to reporting some of the thinly veiled insults being traded between party leaders, they went on to provide mini-biographies of the four 'notable' candidates. These were Winston Churchill (Oldham), Conan Doyle (Edinburgh Central), Captain Lambton (Newcastle) and Gilbert Parker (Gravesend). The paper naturally focused on Conan Doyle's Edinburgh connections. They laid particular emphasis on the city being the location of Conan Doyle's medical training and on the fact that 'the prototype of the immortal "Sherlock Holmes" was one of his teachers.'

The campaign started out well with Conan Doyle obtaining public support from prominent people including his former teacher Dr. Joseph Bell. Bell went so far as to share a platform with Conan Doyle at the Literary Institute in Edinburgh.

However the campaign turned unpleasant with much being made of Conan Doyle's upbringing. A considerable number of posters were put up around the city making much of Conan Doyle's Catholic background and suggested that he was against the Scottish Kirk. Despite a robust denial from Conan Doyle the damage was done. He lost the seat to Brown by 569 votes.

Despite the defeat, Conan Doyle's performance was viewed very highly by the Liberal Unionists who wrote to him at the Reform Club on October 8th. Bizarrely the letter's author, John Boraston, stated 'I am quite sure your fight produced its effect in South Edinburgh.' The seat in question had returned a Liberal Unionist M.P (Sir Andrew Noel Agnew Bt) but this would presumably have been of little comfort to Conan Doyle. The letter went on to state that Conan Doyle had 'fairly won' his political spurs[84].

Conan Doyle was however not quite done with Edinburgh and explored the possibility of legal action over the tactics used against him. He also, as mentioned by him in *Memories and Adventures*, wrote a letter to *The Scotsman* in which he attempted to make his religious position clear. He was however advised not to proceed with any legal challenge and informed Boraston of this. Boraston wrote back on October 18th (the letter is reproduced in Conan Doyle's autobiography) and expressed regret along with his expectation that Conan Doyle would enter parliament 'at no distant date'.

The election over and done with, Conan Doyle was able to turn his attention back to the war in South Africa. On October 25th he attended the annual dinner of the Pall Mall Club in St. James's Square. The event was reported in *The Times* of the following day which gave special prominence to Conan Doyle and the recently elected M.P. Winston Churchill.

Churchill was the main focus of the dinner with the toast being 'welcome home'[85]. In response to the chairman's opening speech he spoke about the many complaints that reports coming from South Africa had been subject to censorship. He maintained, to cheers from the assembled diners, that such censorship was necessary to maintain not only the army's secrets but also to prevent sensational stories reaching the British public that could cause them to suffer unnecessarily.

---

[84] This letter is also held at the British Library and is complete. It is the certain identity of this letter's author that allows us to speculate as to the authorship of the earlier letter from the Liberal Unionist Association.

[85] Churchill had been in South Africa reporting on behalf of the *Morning Post*.

Winston Churchill M.P. (1900)

Churchill drew particular attention to the slanders in the press against officers of the British Army. In particular he highlighted the fact that officers so slandered were not in a position to defend themselves. This, in his opinion, helped to make the case for censorship.

After Churchill and other speakers had addressed the company a toast was made to the guests 'coupled with the name of Dr. Conan Doyle'. This strongly suggests that Conan Doyle was not a member of the club. As whose guest he had attended is not known however it is certainly possible that the Liberal Unionist Association may have had some involvement in arranging Conan Doyle's appearance.

Conan Doyle, like Churchill, spoke in defence of British officers saying that while there were indeed cases of bad officers it was too often the case that one example was held up as representing the whole officer class. Such conduct, he said, 'made his blood boil'. He also spoke out against the many slanders about their Boer opponents. He rejected stories of Boers misusing flags of surrender to lure out enemies as 'absolute calumny' and that to discredit the valour of the Boers was to 'discredit our victory'. He closed his speech and, according to the report the dinner itself, by stating that it was better that the war be fought to its end rather than having a premature peace.

The same day saw the first of a number of reviews of his latest book. *The Times* of October 25th was one of the first. Overall it was positive stating that Conan Doyle had enjoyed 'a considerable measure of success' and that he had produced 'an interesting volume which has reduced more or less to their perspective the many side issues of the campaign which, through the enterprise of the war correspondent and the reaction of the highly strung feelings of the nation, had been given fictitious importance.' The review did remark on the 'many inaccuracies' but went on to declare them largely unimportant.

The Graphic of October 27th took a similar line and opened its review by stating 'until the dispassionate historian of the future sifts down and arranges all the mass of material and conflicting evidence, to Dr. Conan Doyle must be given the credit of having produced by far the best and most comprehensive book on the South African War which has yet appeared'.

Unfortunately the contents of the book did not go unchallenged. The last chapter dealt with Conan Doyle's thoughts on the lessons that could be learned from the conflict and the military reform that should take place. It was perhaps inevitable that some within the military would take exception to being told how to conduct themselves by a humble doctor and author. One Colonel Lonsdale Hale wrote to *The Times* to dismiss Conan Doyle's suggestions, forcing the latter to respond in a letter (written at the Reform Club[86]) that was published on November 1st. In the letter Conan Doyle stated that he was not attempting to 'teach' the army but that he believed that a smaller and better paid army was the future.

He went on to suggest that this reformed army could be backed up by a militia of trained riflemen and stated that he was in the process of setting up a rifle range in Hindhead to train such men. The progress of this would be reported on in the middle of the following year.

Colonel Hale responded through a later issue of the newspaper and was joined in his opposition by another correspondent who chose to go under the pseudonym of 'Custos'. Custos challenged nearly all of Conan Doyle's points and concluded by saying that he realised that 'many of the lessons of the South African war would be misread; but I was not prepared for such dangerously reactionary counsels as those of Dr. Conan Doyle.'

Predictably, Conan Doyle did not let the matter rest and responded in a letter dated November 6th in which he drew attention to the areas where he felt that Colonel Hale and Custos had misunderstood him. *The Times* was not the only paper in which his position was challenged. A letter in *The Westminster Gazette* objected to certain suggestions in his book on the grounds that it was based on an unfinished campaign. Conan Doyle responded (in a letter dated November 12th) by stating 'I make a rule with each fresh impression of my book to make additions and corrections so as to incorporate into it the latest information on the subject. In this way I hope to minimise those objections which he urges.'[87]

---

[86] *Letters to the Press* edited by John Michael Gibson and Richard Lancelyn Green.

[87] Conan Doyle placed advertisements in newspapers regularly seeking up-to-date information for the latest edition. This was still going on two years later with *The Times* of June 9th 1902 containing a request for information from 'officers or their relatives'.

The publication of his book was marked by the Authors' Club who invited him to be guest speaker at a 'house dinner' on November 12th. To much applause he told the assembled members of his experiences and of the heroism of the many people he had encountered. His speech gained him an ally in the form of *The Penny Illustrated Paper and Illustrated Times*. Their issue on November 17th covered his speech and voiced their support for his opinions on training riflemen at home.

The matter rested until December 25th when a letter written by someone calling themselves 'Sick List' appeared in *The Times*. The author stated that he had enjoyed Conan Doyle's book and that his (Conan Doyle's) arguments in the newspapers had been more 'gentlemanly' than Colonel Hale's but that he objected to war correspondents and military critics assuming the 'right of criticism without the responsibility of direction.' He went on to state that many of the army's failings were attributable in whole or in part to the actions of the civilian population and that military efficiency could not happen without an awakening of the 'national spirit' and the acceptance of the fact that the required reform was needed 'outside and not inside the Army.' The final remark quoted and criticised Conan Doyle:

> 'We have a higher national duty than "saying what we believe to be the truth" and I feel certain that in this view I have the concurrence of Dr. Conan Doyle.'

While these exchanges were going on, Conan Doyle organised the formation of his rifle club and was able, at the end of the year, to inform his mother that it had reached sixty members. It was something of which he was very proud and its progress was something he would discuss often over the coming months.

One of Conan Doyle's final letters of the year was to Greenhough Smith at *The Strand*. Given the way the letter ran it seems probable that Smith had written to him to request some stories for the magazine. Conan Doyle responded by stating that he was too busy with his rifle club and the work on the latest edition of his Boer War book. His letter to Smith ended with the words 'Poor Sherlock R.I.P.'[88]

Of course this last part is the most intriguing. Conan Doyle's reference to Holmes could only have been in relation to the written incarnation as William Gillette's play was far from dead and would appear in London before the end of 1901. Therefore we can surmise with reasonable certainty that Smith had asked for some new Holmes stories and Conan Doyle was reminding him kindly but firmly that this was not going to happen.

However, unwelcome or not, it brought Sherlock Holmes back to the front of Conan Doyle's mind and the great detective would be ready to assist when his creator needed him.

---

[88] *Arthur Conan Doyle: A Life in Letters* edited by Jon Lellenberg et al.

1901

The Coincidences of the Baskervilles

The Hound of the Baskervilles is a story that was written in many places. Parts were written in Devon, parts in London and, of course, parts at Undershaw. However its roots lay in Conan Doyle's voyage in July 1900 from Capetown to Southampton during which he spoke at length with a young journalist named Bertram Fletcher Robinson.

By the time the two men arrived back in England they were firm friends and they later made plans to take a golfing holiday together in early 1901.

At this point existing biographical works adopt different timelines depending on the information that was available to their authors. Some suggest that the golfing holiday took place in March but this would seem unlikely as Conan Doyle paid two visits to the Ashdown Park Hotel in Sussex and also visited Edinburgh. The second visit to the Sussex hotel is easy to fix because it encompassed the day of the national census which was March 31st 1901.

Richard Lancelyn Green managed to fix the date of the golfing holiday or, more specifically, the date of a letter written by Conan Doyle while there at Sunday April 28th[89].

Conan Doyle and Robinson stayed in the Norfolk town of Cromer at the Royal Links Hotel. During the course of their

[89] He achieved this by correlating Conan Doyle's letter, diary and account books with the diary of Winston Churchill with whom Conan Doyle dined on April 30th (*The Hound of the Baskervilles - Part One* by Richard Lancelyn Green. The article appeared in the winter 2001 issue of *The Sherlock Holmes Journal*.)

stay Robinson shared with Conan Doyle the various legends about spectral hounds that were common to both his Devon home and the Norfolk area. They would have almost certainly discussed the legend of Black Shuck, the ghostly hound of East Anglia, who was supposedly a regular wanderer along the Norfolk coast on which Cromer was situated.

Bertram Fletcher Robinson (seated centre) and Conan Doyle (3rd from right) on the S.S. Briton (Courtesy of The Sherlock Holmes Journal)

Conan Doyle was clearly inspired by these conversations and he wrote to his mother informing her of his intention to work on 'a real creeper' with Robinson. At the same time he wrote to Greenhough Smith, outlined the basic idea for the story and requested the sum of fifty pounds per thousand words. Smith was firmly told that Robinson's name would feature prominently - essentially joint-billing.

Then something happened. Within the month Conan Doyle again wrote to Greenhough Smith. In his letter he asked if Smith would be prepared to double the rate of payment if Sherlock Holmes became the principal character of the story. One can only imagine the likely delight in the offices of *The Strand* when the letter arrived. Finally, eight years after he had pushed him over the Reichenbach Falls, Conan Doyle was offering a literary resurrection for Sherlock Holmes.

Smith is unlikely to have hesitated over the decision for long. He would have recognised immediately the likely financial rewards of such a story. The public desire for Holmes had not abated in the years since the publication of *The Final Problem* in 1893[90]. However Greenhough Smith's jubilation would have been tempered by the fact that Conan Doyle was offering the new story as a one-off. There would be no permanent rise from the dead for Holmes. The new story was to be an adventure that Watson had dug out of his dispatch box posthumously.

The question that occupied the minds of many a Conan Doyle fan in recent years is what lay behind the story's change of direction. Why did Conan Doyle decide to change the story from a supernatural tale involving a spectral hound to a detective story featuring Sherlock Holmes - a character he had been all too eager to put behind him.

---

[90] This was demonstrated by the sheer number of Holmes imitators that appeared to fill the void. The most prominent example of these being Sexton Blake who first appeared in the same month as *The Final Problem.*

The Royal Links Hotel (rear) and club house in Cromer Norfolk
(Courtesy of The Sherlock Holmes Journal)

One of the reasons put forward is that he and Robinson quickly realised that the supernatural tale simply would not stretch to a full-length novel of some fifty thousand words. Conan Doyle then presumably had the notion of turning the whole idea into a detective story with a supernatural element and approached Greenhough Smith about including Holmes. This decision may have been, at least in part, inspired by Smith's communications with Conan Doyle, towards the end of 1900, which had concluded with Conan Doyle's reference to Holmes. Equally William Gillette's play could easily have been an influence.

Another plausible reason was Robinson's workload. He discovered that his own journalistic and other writing commitments would prevent him being the full partner in the story that both men had originally envisaged. The result of this was that Robinson relegated himself to the role of 'assistant plot-producer' a title he was to repeatedly use to describe himself[91].

However these commitments clearly were not all that pressing as Robinson was able to spend the end of May and early days of June travelling with Conan Doyle around parts of Dartmoor that would later feature in the legendary story[92]. For many of these journeys they were driven by Henry Baskerville, the coachman who, according to most sources, lent his name to the troubled Baronet of the story.

---

[91] The voluntary use of this term by Robinson is one of the many arguments against the conspiracy theories that appeared concerning the authorship of the story.

[92] According to a bibliography of Robinson by Paul Spiring he produced eighteen articles and one poem in the March to August part of 1901. This is the period covering the conception and publication of *The Hound of the Baskervilles*. He was also very likely immersed in the role of editor for the book *Ice Sports* which was published by Ward Lock & Co. on November 19th 1901.

One reasonable explanation is that Robinson used his supposed workload as an excuse to back out of the project once the decision was made to feature Sherlock Holmes. Robinson quite possibly felt uncomfortable about putting his name to a story whose inevitable success would be down in no small part to a character he had nothing to do with[93].

As mentioned, March 31st 1901 saw the national census. This provided one of the first public records of the makeup of the Undershaw household. As we have seen Conan Doyle was absent when it was taken but so also was his wife.

The former was at the Ashdown Park Hotel in the company of his mother Mary and Jean Leckie. Mary Doyle was clearly there as chaperone in an attempt to prevent wagging tongues. The interesting thing about the census record in this instance is that Conan Doyle still listed his profession as 'physician' even though, with the exception of his Boer War service, he had not been in regular practice since 1891.

Louise, meanwhile, was on holiday with her mother in Torquay. One is forced to wonder how much she enjoyed the holiday given that she very likely knew exactly who her husband was with. Conan Doyle, convinced as he was that he was being covert, probably did not give this a second thought.

At Undershaw the census records showed that, of the family, there were only the two children - Mary and Kingsley and their aunt Emily Hawkins. The remainder listed represented the staff.

Aside from Thomas Cleeve and his wife Elizabeth there was Ellen Davis (the 'Cook Dom') and the young housemaid

[93] Robinson was paid sums by Conan Doyle for his contribution to the story in the months following publication. This too indicates that the two men had not fallen out as claimed by some.

Fanny Harris. Resident at the nearby lodge was the coachman George Holden and his wife Sarah[94].

It can be said with some confidence that life in the Conan Doyle household was complicated. For Conan Doyle himself this was the inevitable consequence of combining a busy writing career with his family life and his relationship with Jean Leckie. For Louise it was the result of living with a terminal condition, looking out for her family and keeping up the pretence of being in ignorance of her husband's other life.

However the complications were not confined to the family. The life of the Cleeves was not without its challenges. At around this time the couple almost certainly learned that Elizabeth Cleeve was pregnant and this fact quite possibly influenced Conan Doyle in his later writing[95].

Returning to the beginning of the month, Saturday March 9th saw Conan Doyle give a speech on the Boer War. This speech, which took place at Hindhead Hall, followed the presentation of a silver rose bowl inscribed with the words 'Arthur Conan Doyle, who at a great crisis - in word and in deed - served his country'[96]

According to the coverage given in *The Times* of March 11th there were 'gifts' although the report carried no details of any of the gifts. The presentation was made by Sir Frederick Pollock. Pollock and Conan Doyle were already acquainted

---

[94] According to the census records Sarah Holden was born in Westmorland. This area was represented in Parliament during parts of the 16th and 17th centuries by members of the Musgrave family. Perhaps these were the northern Musgraves referred to in *The Musgrave Ritual* - the Sherlock Holmes adventure published in *The Strand* in 1893.

[95] The point is expanded upon on later in this chapter.

[96] *A Chronology of the life of Sir Arthur Conan Doyle* by Brian Pugh.

through their mutual membership of the Society of Authors. It is not known whether Pollock contributed to the purchase of the bowl but *The Times* named Sir Henry Irving, Professor Alexander Williamson and Henry Arthur Jones as being amongst the donors. Jones was a dramatist but in later life he penned a series of articles in which he attacked H.G. Wells and George Bernard Shaw. It would be interesting to know how Conan Doyle reacted (if indeed he did at all) to one of his acquaintances attacking another[97].

Henry Arthur Jones (date unknown)

In his speech, Conan Doyle defended British troops against charges of farm burning stating that it was hard that

[97] On March 11th 1902 Conan Doyle would be one of many guests at the opening night of Jones' play *The Princess' Nose* at the Duke of York's Theatre (*Daily Express* March 12th 1902).

men risking their lives for the Empire should be slandered and dishonoured. In a characteristic display of balance he was quick to point out that honourable behaviour was also to be expected from the Boers. By way of example he told how the Boer leader had personally assured John Langman of the health of his son Archie when the latter was captured. He concluded by expressing his hope that the war would soon be over.

April 16th saw an article appear in the *Daily Express* regarding the Sherlock Holmes play. William Gillette's run at the Garrick had finished on June 16th 1900 and he had then taken the play on tour between October of that year and March 30th 1901. At this point the American company was handed to fellow actor Cuyler Hastings so that Gillette could focus on bringing the play to Britain on schedule in September[98].

The *Express* article, entitled *"Sherlock Holmes" in London*, began by promising the Lyceum Theatre's shareholders that they need have no fear for the play which had enjoyed 'a sensational success throughout America for two years'[99].

The article praised Gillette for his performance and energy stating him to be unrivalled in these respects. It also informed its readers of the play's scenes of 'nervous intensity'.

In particular they highlighted a scene in which Holmes escapes from a dark room, convincing those also in the room

---

[98] Hastings had in fact been playing Holmes since September 1900. His task had been to take the play to the smaller cities that Gillette had been forced to miss out. He would later take the play to Australia (*Molding the Image: William Gillette as Sherlock Holmes* by Andrew Malec).

[99] In the biography that he wrote about Irving, Bram Stoker stated that he had seen the play's American debut and had reported on its suitability for the Lyceum to Henry Irving. Clearly Irving had no objection to the play being at the Lyceum with someone else in the starring role. He later argued the case for the play with the theatre's management

that he is still there by means of a lit cigar which remained in place thus creating the impression of someone smoking it.

Apparently the press in one city had described the scene as 'impossibly melodramatic' and, subsequently, an editor had sent the head of the local detective force to see the play and pronounce on the scene's absurdity[100]. The article was able to state, with some amusement, that the detective had reported back that he had actually performed the same trick himself with the same success.

Cuyler Hastings - America's second Sherlock Holmes

May saw the serialisation of *The Great Boer War* commence in *The Wide World Magazine*. An advert in *The*

[100] *The Strand* of December 1901 would later identify the *St. Louis Star* as being the source of this mocking report.

Penny Illustrated Paper and Illustrated Times of May 4th promised that the causes and results of the war would be told 'attractively and impartially'. The same serialisation began in the American version of the magazine one month later.

American issue of The Wide World Magazine containing parts 1 and 2 of Conan Doyle's 'The Great Boer War'
(Author's Collection)

Undershaw c1899. The figures on the left are almost certainly family or visitors. The bent figure on the right may well be Thomas Cleeve, Conan Doyle's butler (Copyright the Francis Frith Collection)

Close up of the figure that may be Thomas Cleeve tending to what may be potted plants (Copyright the Francis Frith Collection)

In June 1901 *The Strand* published an article written by Conan Doyle's friend Captain Philip Trevor. Entitled *A British Commando - An Interview with Conan Doyle*, the article was an interview in which Conan Doyle discussed his Undershaw Rifle Club and how he felt such clubs would benefit Britain by providing trained riflemen. This, as we have already seen, was something that Conan Doyle had written about (and argued about) at the end of the previous year following his experiences in South Africa.

Trevor wrote that, en route to Conan Doyle's study to conduct part of the interview, he spotted a number of South African war relics that he had not noticed before. With his host's permission he relocated Conan Doyle's 'Viking chair' to the outside and arranged a host of these curiosities onto it before capturing the image on camera. The resultant image was one of several featured in the article - all of which were taken by Trevor. One of the photographs in particular, which showed Conan Doyle taking aim with a rifle, described him as a 'Field Cornet'. This term was a South African one and had a variety of meanings depending on context. One such meaning defined the 'Field Cornet' as the head of the militia and this was probably how Captain Trevor intended it to be interpreted. It is open to debate as to how many of his British readers would have understood the term.

Trevor gave an insight into his own personality when he wrote that he found the lack of class distinction within the club disturbing. At the same it demonstrated Conan Doyle's somewhat more commendable attitude to be that of treating everyone as equal and rewarding people based on merit.

South African rifles and shells arranged in the grounds of Undershaw on Conan Doyle's 'Viking' chair. (Strand June 1901, author's collection)

In addition to discussing the rifle club the article also touched on the Boer War which was, after all, the reason for its foundation. The article revealed that Conan Doyle, in an effort to get feedback on the even-handedness of *The Great Boer War*, had sent copies to Boer prisoners of war. In the article he stated that he had sent it because 'I felt that I had tried to state their case fairly, and I therefore hoped that they might take a fair view of our own.'

The response from one group of prisoners was reproduced within the article and ran thus:

'To the Camp Commandant.

'I am authorised by the officers of Hut No. 4 to convey to you and to the author, Conan Doyle, Esq., our heartfelt thanks for the work, "Great Boer War," which is a very interesting addition to our library.

'We are, dear Sir,

'Respectfully yours,

'G.C. Amenur,

'Librarian.'

Conan Doyle 'The Field Cornet' taking aim
(Strand June 1901, author's collection)

The targets being fired at. Conan Doyle's position was in front of the house at the rear
(Strand June 1901, author's collection)

It is hard to ascertain the level of sincerity in this communication and the word 'interesting' does not necessarily suggest that the prisoners agreed with the contents of the book. Conan Doyle, however, clearly interpreted it as a positive reaction. It is perhaps a testament to his even-handedness that a sizable amount of the criticism of his book came from individuals in Britain rather than South Africa.

❧

In the middle of June Conan Doyle was staying in London at Morley's Hotel, Trafalgar Square. His reason for being temporarily resident there was that he had a series of cricket engagements at Lord's[101]. It is interesting to note that at this time he was also working on chapters five and six of *The Hound of the Baskervilles*. It is interesting because chapter five contains the scene in which Sir Henry Baskerville becomes enraged at the loss of a boot whilst staying at his London Hotel. These events take place at the fictional Northumberland Hotel but given that Conan Doyle was staying in Morley's at the time it is not unreasonable to speculate that he based the Northumberland on the hotel in which he was then staying[102].

He certainly could not have used a real name for the hotel of his story. As remarked in other works, Conan Doyle rarely named real hotels in his Holmes stories. The Langham Hotel in London was one of the exceptions. He preferred to invent names for hotels where they featured. The reason for this appears to have been that the hotels in his stories, with the

---

[101] *A Chronology Of The Life of Arthur Conan Doyle* by Brian Pugh.

[102] Towards the end of 1900, in a letter to his mother, Conan Doyle had stated that he was somewhat sick of Morley's Hotel and expressed an intention to try the Golden Cross Hotel where Nelson had apparently once stayed. If he was still feeling a little anti-Morley's it would add weight to the idea that it became the Northumberland of the story.

exception of the Langham, often came in for some sort of criticism. In the case of his latest story he was suggesting unambiguously that the staff members of Sir Henry's hotel were dishonest. It is not unreasonable to suggest that had he named an actual hotel its management would not have thanked him for it[103].

It seems that Conan Doyle may have also drawn on real-life when it came to his description of Baskerville Hall's domestic staff. The Barrymores who act as butler and housekeeper could be said to mirror his own servants the Cleeves who, as we have seen, were married and occupied very much the same roles. The fact that Mrs Barrymore has the first name Eliza and Mrs Cleeve's first name was Elizabeth adds weight to this suggestion. In addition the butler Barrymore refers to the presence of a maid in the house and this could be said to represent Conan Doyle's housemaid Fanny Harris.

It is also possible to speculate as to further parallels. When Sir Henry Baskerville first arrives at Baskerville Hall one of his first conversations with Barrymore revolves around the butler's desire for himself and his wife to leave Sir Henry's employment. It is a curious part of the story as it has no real bearing on the plot and the Barrymores are resident for the entire duration of the story. So why did Conan Doyle write it?

A possible answer is that, once again, Conan Doyle was being influenced by real-life events. By this time it is more than likely that Cleeve and his pregnant wife had informed their employer of their impending change in circumstances and its likely effect on the future.

In the modern days of accessible childcare it is all too easy to forget that working-class Victorian families such as the Cleeves would have been dependent on their families for assistance with childcare. Elizabeth Cleeve's family were based in Cambridgeshire so it would have been to Cleeve's

---

[103] This theory is expanded upon in *Close to Holmes* by your present author.

family in Portsmouth that they would have had to turn. The expectation would probably have been that Elizabeth Cleeve would care for her child personally so her days as parlour maid must have been numbered. It is easy to imagine Cleeve discussing the possibility of leaving Conan Doyle's employ and that this situation was, to a certain extent, mirrored in the story[104].

It may be seen as rather tenuous but a look at the Cleeves' marriage certificate suggests either a coincidence or a deliberate use of their history by Conan Doyle. Elizabeth Cleeve's maiden name was Moore and her father's name was John. It is not beyond the bounds of possibility to suggest that Conan Doyle took the name John Moore and made it John Barrymore in much the same way as he could well have taken Elizabeth Moore and made her Eliza Barrymore. It all depends on how much of his employees' history Conan Doyle is likely to have known.

Other biographies have drawn further parallels between the people and events in Conan Doyle's story and real-life. In his recent biography, Andrew Lycett gives an explanation for the origin of the name Vandeleur which is revealed by Holmes as one of the names the villain Stapleton went by before moving to Dartmoor.

Lycett's explanation is that the name was taken from Lieutenant-Colonel Cecil Vandeleur who had fought in the Boer War and been killed in an ambush in 1901. This is backed up by the fact that the Colonel's death was mentioned subsequently in a revised edition of *The Great Boer War*.

However there is another possible connection which, although more tenuous, is worthy of mention.

---

[104] We do not know if the Cleeves actually did leave Conan Doyle's employ but we do know that by the 1911 census, when Conan Doyle had moved to Crowborough in Sussex, the Cleeves were living with their son in Overton in Hampshire. Cleeve was listed as head of household thus indicating that he was not living with his employer. However he was still listed as a butler.

Colonel Vandeleur may well have provided the name for Stapleton but the character's earlier profession, revealed by Holmes as being in charge of a school, is not catered for in this theory. So from where could the idea have sprung?

One of Conan Doyle's fellow residents in Hindhead was George Bernard Shaw and the two men had a famously rocky relationship. It is hard to know how much about each other's backgrounds they knew but there is a parallel between Stapleton's past and that of a man connected to Bernard Shaw.

The possible link lies in Shaw's early life. For some of his early years Bernard Shaw, his father and his mother had shared their home with one George Lee who was Mrs Shaw's singing teacher. When Lee decided that his musical future lay in London he moved out. Shaw's mother later decided to abandon her husband and follow him[105].

Shaw himself had joined them in 1876 where he even ghost wrote Lee's music column in the London paper *The Hornet.* The possible link lies in the fact that George Lee had adopted the middle name of Vandeleur and would later drop the name George altogether and be known simply as Vandeleur Lee.

This history was to cause Shaw some embarrassment later in his life and he began to become concerned how people might interpret his mother's curious living arrangements with Lee.

Therefore Conan Doyle's decision to make part of his villain's background that of a schoolmaster named Vandeleur could have been pure coincidence or it could have been the case that he had learned something of Shaw's history and had decided to make use of it.

Even if it was pure coincidence it may have caused Shaw a few uneasy moments if he ever read the story.

---

[105] *Shaw and the Charlatan Genius* by John O'Donovan.

ॐ

July saw reports appear in the press which alleged ill-treatment of British soldiers by some elements in the Boer army. Conan Doyle sought to defuse the situation in a letter to *The Times* which was published on the 13th.

In the letter he referred to a communication he had received from a Boer officer. The officer in question expressed satisfaction with the fact that Conan Doyle did not describe every 'regrettable' incident on either side where the proper rules of war had not been followed. It was an admirable attempt on Conan Doyle's part to draw attention to the fact that both sides contained what he called 'a certain percentage of brutes' but that this should not be used as an excuse to condemn an entire army or create 'racial hatred'.

The Times of July 18th reported that the Undershaw Rifle Club had become formally affiliated to Britain's National Rifle Association. This official endorsement very likely caused Conan Doyle to feel some measure of personal satisfaction and he may also have felt that it answered, to some extent, those amongst his critics who had questioned his reasons for founding it in the first place.

THE SHADOW OF SHERLOCK HOLMES.

Illustration from The Hound of the Baskervilles
(Author's collection)

SHERLOCK HOLMES!

"The Hound of the Baskervilles,"

Another Adventure of **Sherlock Holmes,**

By **A. CONAN DOYLE.**

This adventure of the great detective, whose reappearance has so long been hoped for, will be found equal, if not superior, in vivid and thrilling interest, to the best of those which first made his name celebrated all over the world.

The STRAND Magazine

August, 1901.

Advert from The Illustrated London News of August 3rd 1901 heralding the imminent arrival of the Hound of the Baskervilles in The Strand (Author's collection)

Holmes on the page and the stage

In August Sherlock Holmes's long-awaited reappearance debuted in *The Strand*. The sense of public anticipation must have been palpable. It is unarguable that *The Hound of the Baskervilles* is the most famous Sherlock Holmes story (and the most often filmed) and has a good claim on being Conan Doyle's most famous story of all.

In a letter sent to his mother, shortly before the first instalment was published, Conan Doyle confided that it was not as good as he had hoped it would be. More important than his opinion was the opinion of the reading public. Would they be disappointed?

The answer was a very clear 'no'. It is arguable that even if the story had been poor the demand for Holmes was so great (and probably enhanced by the Gillette play's success) that it would have been a commercial success regardless of its literary merit. The circulation of *The Strand* was boosted significantly and there must have been a glass or two lifted skywards in the magazine's offices. The publicity that it brought was also useful for the British debut of William Gillette's play.

It is unlikely that many of the readers of the latest Holmes adventure noticed Conan Doyle's small dig at his own creation. In the very first chapter Doctor Mortimer refers to Holmes as 'the second highest expert in Europe' much to the latter's irritation. It was almost as if Conan Doyle was reminding his own creation of his place in the eyes of his creator.

According to Conan Doyle's accounts, the money soon began to come in. In the month the story began serialisation

Conan Doyle recorded two payments (one for each of the first two instalments) totalling over one thousand pounds. The story would continue to bring in large sums throughout 1901 and 1902.

The London debut of the Sherlock Holmes play was only a few weeks away and, according to an article which later appeared in the December issue of *The Strand*, William Gillette arrived in England in August aboard the White Star Line steam ship *Celtic*[106]. An amusing anecdote appeared in the same article to the effect that an employee of the London and North-Western Railway had boarded the ship, soon after it docked, with a message for Gillette whom he had never seen. Upon enquiring of the passengers as to Gillette's physical appearance he was asked if he was familiar with the illustrations that accompanied the Holmes stories in *The Strand.* When he answered in the affirmative he was told to look for Sherlock Holmes as Gillette was, in the opinion of the passengers, the image of the Paget illustrations[107].

The *Daily Express* of August 27th reported that Gillette was rehearsing his play daily at the Lyceum Theatre. However it also reported that he was to trial the play for a week elsewhere before its formal opening. The chosen venue was the Shakespeare Theatre in Liverpool.

However it appears that the *Daily Express* and *The Strand* were partly mistaken. Passenger lists reveal that Gillette was not amongst the *Celtic*'s passengers in August 1901[108]. In fact it would appear that the only man of that name to arrive in Liverpool in August arrived aboard the *Australasia* on the 28th. The ship had commenced its journey in Canada and had sailed to New York, where Gillette had boarded, before making its way to Liverpool.

---

[106] It was the second ship of that name and had launched in April of 1901. Its regular route was between New York and Liverpool.

[107] *Mr William Gillette as Sherlock Holmes* by Harold J. Shepstone (*The Strand* - December 1901).

[108] Source: Ancestry.co.uk.

The Celtic c1907. The ship that did not bring William Gillette to England in 1901 despite the report in The Strand

The *Daily Express*' mistake probably arose from an assumption on their part. It seems reasonably clear that work was indeed going on at the Lyceum in preparation for the play's opening at the time they stated. One is forced to assume that the reporter took it for granted that Gillette had travelled with the rest of his company[109].

The Strand's mistake is harder to account for. Perhaps the article's author assumed that Gillette's ship had commenced its journey in New York (rather than stopping there en route) and saw that the *Celtic* was the only ship that had started from there at the right time. From that point on he said 'Celtic' when he should have said 'Australasia'.

Gillette's late arrival in England did not leave him with much time before his first performance in Liverpool. Whilst it is conceivable (but unlikely) that he could have travelled to London after his arrival and spent a little time at the Lyceum he certainly would not have been able to rehearse there as much as the *Express* had suggested. This lack (or perhaps absence) of rehearsal time was to come back to haunt him.

Gillette's play opened to paying audiences in Liverpool on September 2nd 1901. *The Penny Illustrated Paper and Illustrated Times* of September 7th reported that it had played for the previous week and that its trial run had been 'successful'. Further details were omitted presumably to avoid

[109] Not all of the original American cast transferred to Britain. One of those who did was Harold Heaton who played the role of Sir Edward Leighton. A man by the name H. Heaton, with the occupation of 'traveller', arrived in Southampton, according to passenger lists, aboard the Grosser Kurfürst on August 3rd. On the same ship were listed a Mrs Fealy and a Miss M Fealy. These could well have been Maude Fealy (who had been hired to play Holmes's love interest Alice Faulkner) and her mother although the ages listed were older than would be expected. Inaccurate record keeping or pure coincidence?

detracting from the official London debut. Another reason could have been that a full review would have been inadequate as the Liverpool audiences were almost certainly denied the complete experience.

The play required many special effects and these were costly and complicated to arrange. While the play was being performed in Liverpool the Lyceum Theatre in London was being prepared. According to *The Penny Illustrated Paper and Illustrated Times* of August 24th considerable stage alterations were required 'on account of the extraordinary electrical effects introduced in Mr. William Gillette's version of Dr. Conan Doyle's famous creation'. Given the short run in Liverpool it is likely that the audiences there did not have the benefit of these effects as there would not likely have been the time or inclination to undertake the work for a short preview.

Having completed their Liverpool run Gillette and company headed to London via a special train in time for the Lyceum debut on September 9th[110]. It was widely expected that Conan Doyle would attend the performance and the *Daily Express* of September 9th stated that it was Conan Doyle's intention to do so. However they also remarked that he was not in the best of health and therefore it was uncertain whether or not he would make a speech before or after the performance. The newspaper also remarked that it was Gillette's policy not to rehearse on the day before a debut and that a last minute decision had been made 'to have a new stage'.

At the appointed time, the Lyceum Theatre curtain rose and the play was performed. Amongst the audience many newspapers were represented. These included *The New York Times* and its report was published the next day.

Unhappily for the company and Gillette in particular it was not a perfect night. According to the newspaper a number of hostile audience members began booing from the gallery and

---

[110] A 'special' train was one commissioned by those travelling. Gillette's train arrived in London on September 8th at 2pm (*Daily Express*, September 9th).

did so during each act. When the performance was over and Gillette came forward to make a speech he was compelled to wait in silence at the front of the stage for six minutes while the insults continued.

The New York Times was not the only paper to report this less than perfect opening. The *Daily Express* review, which also appeared on the 10th, ran along very much the same lines. Their reporter began very positively stating that the audience was 'riveted by a succession of sensational situations' and that 'Mr. Gillette won a personal triumph as Holmes'.

Turning to the disruption, the newspaper reported that it was caused by a 'small but noisy minority' whose interruptions were 'strongly resented in all parts of the theatre'.

However, the reporters from these newspapers were clearly not aware of the reason for some of the disruption. One is forced to assume, given the prominence and financial resources of their respective newspapers, that they had excellent seats and enjoyed a good view of the play. The experience was not so good for representatives of other newspapers who had less advantageous seating.

One of these was the reporter who went under the alias 'The Prompter'. This individual worked for *The Penny Illustrated Paper and Illustrated Times*. The newspaper only came out on Saturdays and no doubt had a smaller budget and seated its reporters in less costly seats.

In the edition of the newspaper published on the 14th the reporter stated that the discontent in the upper parts of the theatre was caused by Gillette's inability to speak loudly enough to be heard beyond the stalls. The frustration displayed in the article suggested that this was the reporter's first-hand experience as well as that of others.

He wrote that it was 'irritation at this low level of utterance (a sadly common fault where no excuse exists) that led to the uproar at the finish of "Sherlock Holmes"'. He went on to say:

'While regretting the discourtesy of a small section of the audience, I may seize the opportunity to urge actors and actresses to make their voices heard distinctly. This duty, often neglected by stars to whom the public has been too indulgent, ought surely to be paramount with the acting profession.'

It appears, from his speech at the end of the performance, that Gillette was unaware that he could not be heard. Perhaps, ironically, he was unable to hear any demands for him to speak up. Instead he seems to have been convinced that the audience was objecting to the play itself and criticising Conan Doyle.

Conan Doyle, despite the reports in the press, had not been able to attend so Gillette took it upon himself to defend him.

He stated, according to *The New York Times*, 'Dr. Doyle is absent and in a safer place' and went on to remark on how he had tried his best to present the character in a way his creator would have been happy with. He concluded by saying that he appreciated the audience's praise and felt that he was 'among friends.'[111]

This was not wishful thinking on Gillette's part as, aside from the unhappy gallery, the rest of the audience applauded his efforts. However it seems reasonably clear that it was his lack of rehearsal time at the Lyceum, combined with his policy of not rehearsing the day before a debut, which led him to misjudge the volume of his voice and thus trigger some of the unhappiness in his audience.

The most intensely critical appraisal of his performance came from critic J.T. Grein who wrote his piece on September 15th. Grein's review practically contained a negative in every sentence with examples such as 'It is a penny dreadful minus the coherence which is to be found in even that very cheap product of scribblership.'[112] Gillette's performance was

---

[111] This mention of Conan Doyle's absence places the newspaper report at odds with some sources which stated that both Conan Doyle and Gillette took applause from the stage after the debut performance.

[112] The full review later appeared in *Dramatic Criticism 1900-1901 Volume 3.* The source, in this instance, was a reprint in *The Sherlock Holmes Journal (Winter 1958 Volume 4 Number 1).*

summed up with the line 'The performance will confirm Mr. Gillette's reputation as an actor of great resources, but I fear that at best his fame as an artist will remain unimpaired by his thankless experiment'.

Despite the opinions of Grein the play went on to perform in front of full houses and such was its popularity that *The New York Times* of November 23rd reported that the management of the Lyceum Theatre had negotiated an extension of the play with Charles Frohman. The deal that was arranged ensured that the play continued to run beyond its initial twelve week agreement until Sir Henry Irving returned from America. This meant that the play finished, after two hundred and sixteen performances, on April 12th 1902 which ensured that it left the Lyceum in the same month that the final instalment of *The Hound of the Baskervilles* was published in *The Strand*. In many ways the success of the one assisted with the success of the other given that they had both essentially run in parallel.

Nine days before the play closed Gillette sponsored (and presumably hosted) a farewell dinner at the theatre. Conan Doyle was in Italy visiting Nelson and Ida Foley and was thus unable to attend. Those who did attend included the American Ambassador Joseph Choate, Charles Frohman and both Henry Irving and Herbert Beerbohm Tree[113]. The two actor-managers must have wondered at some point if they would have done so well had either of them secured the play and its lead role a few years earlier.

Gillette then took the play on a short tour of northern England followed by tours of Scotland and Ireland. Finally he returned to Liverpool and performed the play between the 26th and 31st of May 1902 before heading back to the United States[114].

---

[113] *Sherlock Holmes Journal (Spring 1960 Volume 4 Number 4).*

[114] *Moulding the Image: William Gillette as Sherlock Holmes* by Andrew Malec.

SHERLOCK HOLMES. ACT I.

William Gillette as Holmes (1900)
(Author's collection)

The middle of September 1901 saw Conan Doyle make an appearance at the Royal Albert Hall to judge a bodybuilding contest.

The contest was held on September 14th and was entitled the Sandow Competition after the pioneering bodybuilder Eugen Sandow (1867 – 1925)

Eugen Sandow (date unknown)

Conan Doyle's co-judge was Sir Charles Lawes, a prominent rower and sculptor.

Sir Charles Lawes (from Vanity Fair magazine)

The event was a success, with *The Penny Illustrated Paper and Illustrated Times* of September 21st reporting that the event was likely to raise six hundred pounds for the Mansion House Transvaal Relief Fund. The fund had been set up by the Lord

Mayor's office soon after the outbreak of hostilities between the two countries and its primary purpose was to provide funds for the families of British soldiers killed in the conflict.

Conan Doyle's interest in the event was twofold. On the one hand, as stated, the event was to raise money for the fund. The other reason for his interest was that he was something of a fan of Sandow who was regarded as leading the emerging field of bodybuilding. As far back as March of 1898 Conan Doyle had become concerned about his weight. On March 6th of that year he had written the solitary entry '16 Stone' in his diary and by November of that same year he had begun following Sandow's exercise regime. In the entry for November 16th 1898 he noted that his starting weight was fifteen stone and nine pounds.

Whether his interest in his weight was to do with his general fitness or a desire to impress Jean is open to speculation. In all likelihood it was a combination of the two.

In his autobiography, Conan Doyle stated that when he discovered that the competition winner, a man named in the press coverage as W.L. Murray of Nottingham, intended to wander the streets of London with his valuable trophy until the first train home he paid for him to stay at Morley's Hotel where he himself was staying.

The day of the contest also saw the birth of Thomas and Elizabeth Cleeve's son, Rodney John Cleeve, in Horsham. Presumably he was born in Horsham Hospital although this is unconfirmed. However if this supposition is accurate it raises an interesting question. As a private hospital it charged fees to its patients. At the time of Rodney's birth the hospital only had eight beds and must have therefore been in some demand. Its fees are likely to have been beyond the means of Cleeve's wages. Given Conan Doyle's established track record of donating to worthy causes it is possible that he could have contributed towards the medical costs in this case.

Money was certainly of limited concern as the year drew to a close. According to his accounts, Conan Doyle's income for the year was £9947 which was only a little shy of double his income of 1899. Almost all of this increase was down to his Sherlock Holmes related output.

❧

The *Daily Express* of September 24th carried the details of an interview with Conan Doyle concerning the ongoing conflict in South Africa. Optimistically entitled *How to end the War* it concerned his opinions of the renewed Boer fighting.

According to the article the interviewer 'called upon' Conan Doyle although it was not made plain whether this was at Undershaw or elsewhere. Conan Doyle was, at first, unwilling to speak about the campaign but changed his mind when persuaded that his views could be of benefit to the public.

Conan Doyle's opinion was viewed in such glowing terms because, as the article reminded everyone, he had not only been in South Africa but he had also spoken with many of the commanders on the ground. However, arguably the most significant reason was that he was seen as the most even-handed commentator having produced, in his book *The Great Boer War*, a work 'acknowledged by both Boers and Britons to be as fair and accurate as he could make it'.

Conan Doyle's decision to cooperate was not only driven by the entreaties of the reporter. As he admitted in the resultant article, he was hoping to bring out a new edition of his book which would cover 'all operations up to the end of the second year of the war'.

Conan Doyle's suggestion for ending the war involved cutting off the head of the snake. By this he referred to the two governments in place in South Africa. He suggested organising the capture of the government principals as the best way to a swift peace. He concluded by criticising the attitude of some Britons saying that there was 'too much of an air of levity sometimes'. In particular he objected to the use of sporting terms in official despatches. A cricket team from South Africa had visited Britain that year on a tour against various English county teams. Certain elements of the British press had been amused at this and had stated, according to Conan Doyle, that 'men could be justified in leaving their own country when it was invaded in order to play cricket.'[115]

When pressed on how long the war could be expected to last he said 'It is mathematically certain that six months must see the end unless there should be a general Cape rising...But who dare prophesy after our fiascos in the past?'

His prophesy was not all that inaccurate as the war ran for another eight months ending with the signing of the Treaty of Vereeniging on May 31st 1902.

❧

The Times of October 28th carried an advertisement concerning the firm Raphael Tuck and Sons Limited. The firm, which had begun operation in the middle of the previous century, had rapidly become a major force competing with the great firms of continental Europe that specialised in the printing and distribution of artistic prints and postcards.

The advertisement announced the company's transition into a company limited by shares and made it clear that the shares were available for purchase by the general public. It was notable as Conan Doyle was listed as one of the five directors of the firm and one of only two non-Tuck family members.

December 6th saw Conan Doyle in Edinburgh for the annual Walter Scott Club dinner[116]. He took advantage of the occasion to advise his audience to 'take refuge in the more restful literature of the past.' He said it was the only antidote to the 'scrappy literature of the present - the literature of St Vitus's

[115] Conan Doyle disagreed with this most strongly and had written a letter to *The Spectator* (published April 20th) to that effect when news of the cricket tour was announced.
[116] *Daily Express* December 7th 1901.

dance'. Given his general even-handedness it is reasonable to suppose that he placed his own works (especially Sherlock Holmes) into this category as much as those of his other contemporaries[117].

[117] In 1959 the president of the club was Hesketh Pearson. Amongst Pearson's many works was one of the earliest biographies of Conan Doyle - *Conan Doyle: His Life and Art* - which had been published in 1943. Source: The Edinburgh Sir Walter Scott Club.

1902

Titles and glory

Conan Doyle merited a brief mention in the press in the opening days of 1902. Allegations of crimes enacted by British soldiers against Boer women and girls were circulating in the German press and causing a certain amount of unrest there and around the world.

The allegations were hardly insignificant. The *Daily Express* reported that the principal allegation was that 'Boer girls from twelve years old upward have been removed, systematically and wholesale, from the Irene concentration camp to Pretoria for shameful purposes'[118].

The newspaper made clear its disgust at the reports by stating that they had originated from 'sundry Boer and pro-Boer scoundrels who claim to have seen these things with their own eyes'.

In an effort to counter some of this ill-feeling the newspaper communicated with Lord Roberts who naturally repudiated the allegations. The newspaper stated that his assurance was welcome and further stated 'we are glad Dr. Conan Doyle is busy upon a refutation in five European languages, which he will send to every deputy, statesman, and newspaper in the countries where these atrocious calumnies have been circulated.'

---

[118] The article was entitled *The Lie Direct* and appeared in the January 4th issue.

By January 16th the work entitled *The War in South Africa: Its Cause and Conduct* was available in Britain published by Smith, Elder & Co[119].

The *Daily Express* of that date welcomed its publication and quoted Conan Doyle's preface 'For some reason, which may be either arrogance or apathy, the British are very slow to state their case to the world'.

This then was Conan Doyle performing that role on behalf of his country. However it was only Britain that was destined to see his book unless money could be found to fund translation into other languages and publishers found to print and distribute it. Hence the article also requested that Britons donate money for those purposes.

Copies of the English version still made it abroad and began to impress people in favour of the British position. One of the earliest results of this came in February 1902 when the *Daily Express* of February 13th was able to report that the Nova Scotia Historical Society had awarded Conan Doyle life membership for 'his patriotic work for the Empire'.

By the end of March the necessary monies had clearly been secured to fund the desired translations and *The Times* of March 26th was able to print an advert from Smith, Elder & Co. which listed the addresses of publishers throughout the world that could or would eventually be supplying the book. Such was the demand that even a Braille version was produced and such was the patriotic effort that George Newnes agreed to help distribute copies despite not being the book's British publisher.

The *Daily Express* of the same date elected to focus on Conan Doyle's fictional output. March 25th had seen the publication of the hardcover edition of *The Hound of the Baskervilles* and the newspaper reviewed the book on page four. They began by stating 'Since the day when Dr. Conan

[119] Conan Doyle had clearly sent the mam a copy of his work during its composition. She was bold enough to make suggestions for corrections. (Source: Letter at British Library).

Doyle wrote "The Final Problem" and the waters of the mountain torrent closed over the head of Mr. Sherlock Holmes, posterity has confirmed the ruling which placed Sherlock Holmes as the greatest detective of whom we have record.'

The author of the article then showed remarkable foresight by stating 'Sherlock Holmes began life as a character in fiction. He then became a national institution. He may become a solar myth.'

Due acknowledgement was also made to Bertram Fletcher Robinson with the paper stating that readers owed Robinson for the story to a 'considerable extent'. They also quoted Conan Doyle's dedication and concluded, after an outline of the plot, that people were unlikely to grow tired of Holmes.

It was on April 12th that the newspaper decided to join the discussion on Conan Doyle's Boer War output. The issue of that day carried an article entitled *Slander Run to Earth - How Dr. Conan Doyle Hunted Down Boer Libels*. It opened with a quote from a letter which had been sent to Conan Doyle by one reader. Conan Doyle had received a number of these since publication and he was delighted to report that the highlighted letter had opened with 'I am heartily ashamed of myself to think that I should ever have thought so ill of my own fellow-countrymen.'

The article also stated that in excess of three hundred thousand copies of Conan Doyle's latest effort had been distributed in Britain with an additional ten thousand in the Welsh language. The only country in Europe in which distribution was yet to take place was the Netherlands where, Conan Doyle stated, there were 'considerable difficulties which we will overcome'.

He also took the opportunity to confess to some small inaccuracies within his book but that these were limited to a few minor misquotations and a 'technical confusion between expansive and explosive ammunition.'

The clear success of the book in going some way to transforming international opinion in favour of Britain caused those in power to start considering the idea of honouring

Conan Doyle. The rumours to this effect quickly reached him and he was decidedly uncomfortable about it. As in all such cases of personal crisis he turned to his mother. Regrettably for him his mother, on this matter, was destined to be his opponent rather than his ally.

In a series of letters on the subject, Conan Doyle repeatedly stated his opposition to a knighthood, which he viewed as the most likely honour to be offered, seeing it as something not appropriate for someone in his position. This was Conan Doyle's way of pointing out that, amongst the writing fraternity, it was generally seen as something not to be desired.

The mam, on the other hand, was highly enthusiastic about the prospect of her son being knighted and consequently did not offer him the support he expected from her. When he was formally notified that a knighthood was indeed being proposed his initial inclination to refuse it was only halted when his mother pointed out that doing so would be an insult to the King with whom Conan Doyle had dined not long before[120].

So, despite his strong misgivings, Conan Doyle decided to accept the honour. As a man who was always sensitive to the happiness and security of his family (with the possible exception at this point of his wife) he probably accepted the honour as much to please them as to avoid insulting King Edward[121].

---

[120] *Arthur Conan Doyle: A Life in Letters* edited by Jon Lellenberg et al.

[121] In 1924 Conan Doyle was able to vent his discomfort about his knighthood. In his Sherlock Holmes story *The Adventure of the Three Garridebs*, Watson recalls the events of the story by mentioning that they took place towards the end of June 1902 and that he remembered it so well because it was the same time that Sherlock Holmes refused a knighthood for 'services which may perhaps some day be described'. The date was a clear reference to Conan Doyle's own knighthood and, given his volatile relationship with his most famous character, it is possible that he rather enjoyed depriving Holmes of such an honour.

The announcement of the honour was made soon afterwards in *The Times* of June 26th although the investiture was to take place later in the year. The *Daily Express* of the following day under the misleading title of *Members of the new "Order of Merit"* carried small portraits of a select few of the men due to receive honours that year. The article was misleading as not all the men featured were going to receive the eponymous award which had been created that year by the King. Unsurprisingly a number of the recipients of honours were being honoured for their service in the war. Lords Roberts and Kitchener were both reported as due to receive the Order of Merit with the former claiming the honour of being the very first recipient.

William Brodrick, the 8th Viscount Midleton and Lord Lieutenant of Surrey in 1902 (from Vanity Fair)

For Conan Doyle the honours did not stop there. At almost the same time he accepted the position of Deputy Lieutenant of Surrey. This largely ceremonial position was offered to him by the serving Lord-Lieutenant of Surrey, William Brodrick, the 8th Viscount Midleton.

Conan Doyle in his uniform as Deputy Lieutenant of Surrey (Courtesy of Mrs Georgina Doyle)

❧

Conan Doyle resumed his cricketing commitments as soon as time permitted. The *Daily Express* of July 1st reported on the results of a match played the previous day. It was billed as Artists versus Authors and was held at the ground at Esher, Surrey.

Unfortunately for the authors, who included E.W. Hornung as captain, it was something of a rout with the artists winning the match with, at 220 runs, almost double the runs of the authors' total of 112.

The middle of the month saw Conan Doyle back in Crystal Palace representing the MCC against W.G. Grace's London County side. He and Grace faced each other on July 16th and the results were reported in *The Times* of the following day.

In contrast to the match in 1900 Conan Doyle did well and made forty-three runs before having his wicket claimed by Grace. This presumably unsettled Conan Doyle as he was bowled out for nought in his second innings.

July 28th afforded Conan Doyle his first opportunity to speak publicly about his knighthood. The Authors' Club (of which he was chairman) held a dinner in honour of him and two other members who had recently received similar awards. Henry Rider Haggard presided over the event, which was reported in *The Times* of the following day.

In front of an audience which included John Langman, Haggard reminded those assembled of the achievements of the three men. When it came to Conan Doyle Haggard pointed out that while everyone knew his books he was responsible for so much more. His work as a doctor, his service in South Africa and his composition of two notable works on the war were all responsible for the high esteem with which the club's members and the nation at large regarded him. The speech was met with loud cheers.

Conan Doyle suffers W.G. Grace's 'vengeance'
Westminster Libraries; Sherlock Holmes Collection, Marylebone Library

H. Rider Haggard
(Date unknown)

The three men then each spoke in reply with Conan Doyle the last. His initial remarks were to state that he valued 'the approbation of his fellow writing men more than that of any other men in the world.' He went on to tell the assembled company, much to their amusement, of an event which had seen him receive a bill from his gunsmith addressed to 'Sir Sherlock Holmes'. In response to this bill he told how he had written an indignant letter to the gunsmith threatening the withdrawal of his custom only to be told by the man responsible that he had addressed him in that style as he had been reliably informed that men when knighted changed their names and he had been told that Sir Sherlock Holmes was the name Conan Doyle intended to go by.

The *Daily Express* of the same day also carried a report on the dinner and their article stated that Conan Doyle had said that the gunsmith episode was 'almost the first intimation' he had had that he was to be knighted. One would hope that the first came from Buckingham Palace.

Conan Doyle concluded with some remarks regarding the inception of his recent work on the war and acknowledged that it was this that was most likely the reason behind his knighthood. He told his audience how he first conceived the idea on a train to London while reading some of the accusations against the army in the newspapers. He went on to say that in his life fate had often taken a hand and on the very same evening as his train journey he had found himself dining in town next to a stranger to whom he had spoken about his idea. This stranger, who he did not name, had ultimately offered to secure one thousand pounds towards the cost of the project and also turned out to have the necessary connections to put Conan Doyle in touch with translators and others who could assist.

His concluding remark was to state that if his work convinced anyone of how nobly the army had behaved he would consider it the best thing he had ever done.

In the five years since Conan Doyle had met and fallen in love with Jean Leckie the only family member whose support he had been able to rely on had been his mother. Therefore it was naturally to her that his most candid letters were written on the subject of his personal life[122].

He was still deluding himself about the innocence of his relationship with Jean and Louise's supposed ignorance of it but, perhaps in frustration over the unwillingness of certain family members to see things the way he did, he began to justify himself by pointing to examples of what he saw as Louise's failings as a wife.

---

[122] His confidence in his mother's support and discretion was such that he even forwarded letters, sent to him by Jean, to her to read.

He knew that most of the family adored Louise so his arguments and self-justification were confined to his mother whose acceptance of them was almost guaranteed.

The most depressing example of this was a letter dated August 16th[123]. In it he stated that he could no longer give his wife his full love and that the situation was destined to remain that way.

In an attempt to illustrate his position he dragged out an example that even he was forced to admit was absurd. He mentioned an occasion (presumably quite recent) where he had discovered that several of his pipes had been cleaned. He assumed this to be a kindness of Louise and went to thank her. He reported that he was profoundly disappointed when she informed him that they had been cleaned by the boot boy. The fact that she had not personally performed this service allowed Conan Doyle to feel at least partly justified in his reduced affection for his wife.

In August and September Conan Doyle wrote to his mother about trips he was making to Devon. On both occasions Jean joined him there. In his letters Conan Doyle spoke of his plans to take Jean on a tour of the areas that had inspired parts of *The Hound of the Baskervilles*. On the first of these visits to the county Conan Doyle boasted that he had managed to secure a position for Jean's younger brother Robert with Sir George Newnes. He quoted the salary to his mother and joked that the way he had sorted out the life of Robert Leckie made up for the fact that he had messed up or 'twisted' the life of Jean. It did not seem to occur to him that it was his own life was that was being mangled in his efforts to please everyone.

On the occasion of his second visit in September Conan Doyle was involved in the unveiling of a bust of Sir George Newnes at Lynton. The event was reported in *The Times* of September 9th. Newnes had been Conan Doyle's long time

---

[123] *Arthur Conan Doyle: A Life in Letters* edited by Jon Lellenberg et al.

supporter and publisher and naturally Conan Doyle took a prominent part in events. In his speech he remarked upon the effort Newnes had made to bring quality literature to the masses of people who had benefited from the educational reforms some thirty years previously and how the work now available in this country was far superior to that available in some European countries.

October 24th saw the day that Conan Doyle had not wanted to see. In the days before he had written to his mother and explained how events were to unfold and which members of the family were to be there. It seems that he was trying his best to persuade his mother to attend. Given that she was the one person who had pushed more than any other for him to accept the honour it is strange that she should not wish to see it conferred.

Ultimately, the Hornungs and the Angells[124] along with Louise and the children were those who saw him knighted. Conan Doyle wrote again to his mother the following day to let her know of the family dinner that was held that evening in celebration. *The Times* reported on the event in the next day's issue.

---

[124] Revd Charles Cyril Angell had married Conan Doyle's sister Mary (Dodo) in April 1899.

1903

'I am glad to stretch myself, Watson'

The year 1903 was a momentous one for fans of Conan Doyle's work. *The Hound of the Baskervilles* had performed beyond the wildest dreams (and probably expectations) of all concerned and the pressure for a full-time return of Sherlock Holmes continued to build.

Despite this Conan Doyle was not inclined to succumb. The fact that he ultimately did so was down to one man - his name was Norman Hapgood.

Hapgood (1868 - 1937) was the relatively new editor of the American magazine *Collier's Weekly* and, perhaps eager for an early coup in his reign, he approached Conan Doyle in March with a request for some new Sherlock Holmes adventures.

At this point it appears that Conan Doyle returned to the type of bargaining that he had conducted with Greenhough Smith at *The Strand* a little over a decade earlier. When Hapgood sought world rights for six new Holmes stories at six thousand pounds Conan Doyle responded by offering him just the American rights for the same amount.

Was Conan Doyle playing the same game as he had before? Was he deliberately offering Hapgood poorer terms than he sought in an effort to kill the whole idea? It is probably not easy to determine this for certain but Conan Doyle clearly enjoyed the whole process. He remarked in a letter to his brother Innes that he had enjoyed the negotiations.

A typical issue of Collier's Weekly (July 29th 1897)

Ultimately the money became too much to resist. Hapgood was evidently determined to get the stories he wanted and his final offer was twenty-five thousand dollars for six stories, thirty-thousand dollars for eight or forty-five thousand dollars for twelve. The offer was purely for the American rights and was irrespective of story length. Conan Doyle finally gave in and agreed with the concise response 'Very well, A.C D.'[125].

Holmes was to live again.

Although it was not stated clearly in the letters that are accessible today, it is clear from the reports that followed that Conan Doyle had agreed to write eight new stories.

At this point Hapgood's employer, Peter Fenelon Collier, decided to go public in England. The *Daily Express* of March 25th carried an article entitled *Another Invasion.* In it Collier announced his intention to start printing his magazine in the United Kingdom despite the failure of other American magazines that had attempted to establish themselves in the market.

He went on to boast about the superiority of his presses to those available anywhere in England and how he would be able to produce a magazine containing no less than sixteen pages in colour in comparison to the best in England which could manage only eight.

His boasting continued, detailing the larger number of correspondents that he was able to place around the world and the amount of money that he had at his disposal. His ultimate boast was to state that he had 'just paid Sir Conan Doyle £6,000 for eight stories which will appear in 'Collier's'[126].

Interestingly he failed to state what stories he had paid for and this was presumably because of his failure to secure rights outside of America. Although he would have clearly loved to have been able to announce that it was his money that had brought about the successful resurrection of Sherlock Holmes

---

[125] *The Life of Sir Arthur Conan Doyle* by John Dickson Carr.

[126] According to the exchange rate at the time £6000 was roughly equivalent to $30,000. (Source *measuringworth.com*)

he knew that this news would be of little interest to his potential British readership as they would not get to read them in his magazine. It was presumably considered better not to mention Holmes at all rather than alert people in Britain to the fact that the stories they really craved were destined to appear in the magazine of one of his competitors. Had he done so he would have effectively been promoting *The Strand* at his own expense.

Norman Hapgood - editor of Collier's Weekly (1903 - 1912) c1900

From Conan Doyle's perspective this 'divide and conquer' approach was very sensible. He knew that he would be able to secure similarly generous terms with publications in other countries. The inevitable negotiations with *The Strand* were likely to have been just as entertaining for him as they had been with *Collier's*. Greenhough Smith and George Newnes would have very likely paid whatever they were asked knowing as they did that the stories were guaranteed to make them more money than they cost to secure. Whether Smith felt in any way aggrieved that Hapgood and Collier had succeeded where had had failed is unknown but one can easily imagine that he was slightly put out.

Reaction in the family was mixed. Innes was pleased and responded 'Good old Sherlock. I think he has had quite a long enough rest.' Conan Doyle's mother was not so enthusiastic and expressed these feelings to her son who was forced to pen a letter to her in which he attempted to reassure her that he was still up to the task of crafting fresh stories.

The irony of course was that Mary Doyle was the most vocal opponent of her son's original decision to bring Holmes to an end. When he had first toyed with the idea for the conclusion of the very first series of stories in 1892 she had dissuaded him and suggested an idea that later gave rise to the story entitled *The Copper Beeches*. She later attempted to stop him putting an end to Holmes at the end of the second series - this time without success. Quite why she had reservations about Holmes's resurrection at this point is difficult to determine. Is it possible that her concern lay in her opinion of *The Hound of the Baskervilles*? Conan Doyle had said to her himself that he was not entirely happy with it. Perhaps it was an opinion she shared and which led her to be concerned about the likely quality of future stories.

By March 31st Conan Doyle had written the first of these stories - *The Empty House*[127]. It was not a classic example but this was largely down to the fact that the story had to serve two purposes. Firstly it had to feature a puzzle for Holmes to solve but it also had to explain Holmes's resurrection. Conan Doyle

---

[127] Source: Conan Doyle's diary for 1903.

recognised that the explanation for Holmes's disappearance and reappearance would be the primary interest for his readers so the greater effort went into that part of the story. The actual crime (the murder of Ronald Adair) got considerably less attention and was not much more than a sideshow.

The next two stories swiftly followed. These were *The Norwood Builder* and *The Solitary Cyclist* which were completed on April 15th and 27th respectively[128]. At this point Conan Doyle put Holmes to one side in order to host a shooting competition at Undershaw. This was held on Saturday May 2nd and involved the members of clubs from all over Surrey and the south-east. Conan Doyle's home team consisted of the landlord and barman from 'the village inn', a 'working electrical engineer' and himself[129]. They ended up coming second by one point to a team from the London and South Western Railway Club.

This pleasant diversion over Conan Doyle focused his attention back on Sherlock Holmes and some criticisms he had received from Greenhough Smith. Smith was not happy with the latest two stories primarily on the grounds that they featured no real crimes of note. In other words - he wanted some murders.

Conan Doyle rejected the criticisms of *The Norwood Builder* but accepted that *The Solitary Cyclist* needed work and spent part of May trying to improve it but he eventually gave up admitting to Greenhough Smith that it was a good story that was let down by the denouement and the fact that Holmes had little hand in how events unfolded. He put it to one side and got on with the next in the series, *The Dancing Men*, which he completed on June 3rd. This story featured the murder that Smith clearly longed for and Conan Doyle suggested that it be used to break up the earlier tame stories[130].

---

[128] Source: Conan Doyle's diary for 1903.

[129] *The Times* May 4th 1903.

[130] This was ultimately done with *The Dancing Men* being published between *The Norwood Builder* and *The Solitary Cyclist. The Dancing*

The curious aspect about all this was that, despite the fact that the original deal to resurrect Holmes was struck with Hapgood and *Collier's Weekly*, Conan Doyle was discussing story quality and publication order with Greenhough Smith and effectively allowing Smith's opinion to influence his output.

In an earlier letter dated May 14th, written to Smith, Conan Doyle stated that 'the Americans', presumably Hapgood and Collier, had been trying to persuade him to write twelve stories instead of the agreed eight. He went on to say that he would stick to the original number in accordance with Smith's advice.

It is interesting to speculate what Hapgood would have thought of this decision making going on behind his back, especially when Smith was encouraging Conan Doyle not to do something that he, Hapgood, really wanted him to do. For Smith, the fact that he was managing to exert this influence may well have made up for any grievance he may have conceivably felt for not managing to bring about Holmes's resurrection himself. However it shows Smith's lack of faith in the new stories that he was actually encouraging Conan Doyle not to write additional adventures when more stories would have meant more sales and revenue for *The Strand.*

The influence of Jean Leckie on the new stories is unmistakable. Conan Doyle stated that Jean had given him the idea for *The Empty House* although the extent of her input is debatable. Conan Doyle's feelings for her were such that he could very well have, consciously or not, exaggerated her involvement.

The Norwood Builder featured the character of John Hector MacFarlane whose family lived in Blackheath. It was clearly no coincidence that this is where Jean's family came from. The story also allowed Conan Doyle to wallow in a little nostalgia by revisiting some of the familiar locations from his

---

Men was written in Norfolk where Conan Doyle was then staying. His hosts, the Cubitt family, provided the surname of Holmes's client.

past. His decision to feature the Anerley Arms Hotel makes this clear[131].

The sixth story in the series, entitled *Black Peter,* was set in Forest Row in Sussex, only a short distance from the Ashdown Park Hotel in which Conan Doyle and Jean had stayed at the time of the 1901 census. He completed the story on July 26th and began work on the next - *Charles Augustus Milverton.* During this period the American press decided to run a story suggesting that the series would run for more than eight stories.

The New York Times of August 1st stated that there would be 'all in all a baker's dozen of episodes'. Curiously they also suggested that the first story was still being edited and stated that Conan Doyle was still to decide exactly how Holmes was to be resurrected. According to them the decision was yet to be made as to whether Holmes was to come back from the dead or whether these new stories would, like *The Hound of the Baskervilles*, be posthumous stories from Watson's dispatch box.

Now most of this was clearly speculation as Conan Doyle was still in the process of writing the seventh story (which he would finish five days after the publication of the article) and was yet to begin the eighth. The fact that he had certainly not undertaken to write more than eight is clear from the ending of the eighth in the series, *The Six Napoleons,* which he completed on September 15th. The story concludes with the following speech from Inspector Lestrade:

'We're not jealous of you at Scotland Yard. No, sir, we are very proud of you, and if you come down to-morrow there's not a man,

---

[131] As mentioned in the chapter on 1900 this hotel may have been used by Conan Doyle when he was in the area playing cricket against London County. He may also have used it during his Norwood residency in connection with his membership of the Norwood Cricket Club.

from the oldest inspector to the youngest constable, who wouldn't be glad to shake you by the hand.'

This was clearly intended to draw a line under Holmes's adventures. However, following the completion of the eighth story some further negotiations clearly took place resulting in Conan Doyle agreeing to a further four stories - taking the series to twelve. The first of the next batch, and the ninth of the series, *The Three Students*, was completed on November 9th. The 'baker's dozen' referred to in the American press remained speculation as Conan Doyle would ultimately not make a decision on whether or not to write a thirteenth until May 1904[132].

The fact that Conan Doyle was busy with the new series of stories showed when he did not attend the wedding in July 1903 of Anthony Hope. The notion that he was invited is suggested by the fact that Louise Conan Doyle was listed amongst the guests and it is unlikely that she would have been invited alone[133]. Hope, who today is most famous for his book *The Prisoner of Zenda*, married Elizabeth Somerville Sheldon who, at twenty, was half his age. Elizabeth was American and counted amongst her friends the young actress Ethel Barrymore who was one of three bridesmaids[134].

---

[132] *Conan Doyle: The Man Who Created Sherlock Holmes* by Andrew Lycett.

[133] *Daily Express* July 2nd 1903.

[134] As an illustration of the interconnection between many of the people linked, however tenuously, to Conan Doyle, it is interesting to note that Ethel Barrymore was the sister of John Barrymore who went on to play Sherlock Holmes in the 1922 silent film of the same name. She was also friends, in later life, with Henry Daniell, who played Moriarty more than once opposite Basil Rathbone, and Louis Calhern, who played Colonel Zapt in the 1952 film version of *The Prisoner of Zenda.* The film starred Stewart Granger who would eventually also portray Sherlock Holmes in a 1972 television film of *The Hound of the Baskervilles.*

By the end of July Conan Doyle's workload had clearly eased as he was able to attend the Atlantic Union Banquet at the Hotel Cecil on the 28th. The *Daily Express* of the following day carried a very concise report on the event which concentrated solely on part of Conan Doyle's speech. The article reported Conan Doyle as saying that Britain was undergoing a 'quiet annexation' by America. Devoid of context as the article was it is difficult to know whether Conan Doyle was expressing this as a good or bad thing. However his reference to a 'world-wide country under a flag which shall be a quartering of the Union Jack with the Stars and Stripes' in his 1892 Holmes adventure *The Noble Bachelor* would suggest he saw it, to a certain extent at least, in a positive light.

Anthony Hope. Author of The Prisoner of Zenda

August saw a rather interesting article appear in the pages of the *Daily Express*. It demonstrated that Conan Doyle was already spending some of his recently acquired wealth. In the newspaper's issue of August 14th an article entitled *Statues while you wait* detailed how Conan Doyle and a man by the name of W.G. Jones had patented a device called the Sculptograph.

The device essentially enabled the swift copying of statues as well as other items and had been invented in Naples by a man named Bontempi. According to the article Conan Doyle had spent 'a large sum of money in bringing the original Sculptograph over from Italy, and securing the entire rights'. The article also mentioned that noted sculptor Thomas Brock had inspected the device, presumably at Conan Doyle's invitation, and was of the opinion that it would revolutionise the art of sculpture.

What is not known is exactly how long Conan Doyle had been in negotiations over the device or indeed how he had first become aware of it. However it is interesting to speculate whether the knowledge of this device and its purpose had any influence on his story *The Six Napoleons* and its mass produced busts of Napoleon or if it was the other way round.

The new Holmes series, eventually dubbed *The Return of Sherlock Holmes*, debuted in *Collier's Weekly* in September. In Britain the press was in no mood to wait and began discussing *The Empty House* before its publication in *The Strand* the following month.

The *Daily Express* of September 30th discussed the story in an article entitled *Sherlock Revived* with the rhyming subtitle *The Great Detective Never Died*. The article essentially gave away over half the story by stating what had happened to Holmes and even quoted some of the story's text. The only part not discussed in detail was the murder which had brought Holmes back to London and into the lives of his readers.

Thomas Brock R.A. (1847 - 1922)

What, if anything, George Newnes and Herbert Greenhough Smith thought about this is unknown. It is doubtful however that they feared any negative impact on sales would be caused by the article.

In Britain, *The Strand* ran the stories one month behind *Collier's Weekly* until after the publication of *The Six Napoleons* in April 1904 (May 1904 in *The Strand*).

At this point the management of *Collier's Weekly* elected to pause. They decided that the final four stories (they were not aware of any plans for a thirteenth) would be published in the four months leading up to Christmas 1904. This would ensure that, what they believed to be, Holmes's last adventure would take the form of a Christmas present to their readers.

Greenhough Smith did not feel the same way and carried on publishing. Consequently, when *Collier's Weekly* resumed publication in September 1904 with *The Three Students*, readers in Britain were already reading Holmes's 'last' adventure *The Abbey Grange*.

The year closed with Conan Doyle attending, on December 17th, the centenary of the founding of the waxwork museum Madam Tussaud's. The event was chaired by the literary critic Clement Shorter and attended by other famous names such as J. Comyns-Carr. It is not clear whether Conan Doyle had had much to do with either man prior to this event but he and Comyns-Carr shared two notable acquaintances in the persons of Herbert Beerbohm Tree and Henry Irving.

John Theodore Tussaud, the founder's great-grandson, represented the family and regaled the assembled company with the story of the company's foundation and attempted, perhaps in vain, to quash the rumour that he had a standing offer of a reward payable to anyone capable of enduring an entire night in the Chamber of Horrors. He was at a loss as to how the rumour had arisen and expressed a sincere desire to find out. If Conan Doyle spoke at the event it was not reported[135].

Possibly the final mention of Conan Doyle in the press that year was a brief article in *The Daily Mirror*. In a section entitled *Readers' Parliament* a J. Landfear Lucas of the Junior Constitutional Club in Piccadilly discussed the fact that it was a habit in the country to record and publish the winter sunshine hours in places of high altitude such as Harrogate. Lucas expressed his astonishment that Hindhead, at nearly 850 feet higher than Harrogate, was overlooked for such records.

Clement Shorter and J. Comyns-Carr (from Vanity Fair)

[135] The story was reported in the December 18th issue of *The Daily Mirror.*

His letter contained, what was effectively, a personal plea to Conan Doyle and other 'well-known Hindhead residents' to assist with his aim of getting regular records to be taken in the district. He assured the newspapers readers that they would be 'of a most striking character'. It is unclear whether Conan Doyle took up this particular cause.

1904

Hindhead Golf Club

The Daily Mirror of January 19th reported that Conan Doyle, the Duke of Westminster and others had attended Westminster City Hall the previous day and been elected to the committee in charge of a testimonial fund in honour of one William Melville.

Melville had retired from Special Branch the previous November where he had headed up the department that battled the Irish Fenians and later anarchists. The aim of the committee was to raise funds to enable a grateful nation 'to do something substantial to assist him'[136].

One of the other members of the committee was William Burdett-Coutts, the M.P. for Westminster. It was Burdett-Coutts' claims about the poor state of military hospitals during the Boer War that had contributed to Conan Doyle being required to address the public inquiry in 1900. It is tempting to speculate how the two men would have cooperated given their opposite positions on that issue.

March 15th was an important date to Conan Doyle. So significant was it that it merited a special letter to his mother the following day. It was important as it marked seven years to the day that he and Jean Leckie had been, in their eyes, a couple. Throughout the letter, he wrote about Jean as if she were already his wife. Another example, if more were needed,

[136] Melville's retirement was short-lived. He eventually became involved in the early days of Britain's modern secret service and it has been suggested that it was from him that the codename 'M', as used in the James Bond stories, originated.

of how he simply could not, or would not, recognise how tactless his conduct was.

In the letter he alluded to the awkwardness of the situation and the difficulties that their relationship caused for both Jean and himself. Regardless of your admiration for his work and achievements, your admiration for the man himself cannot help but be reduced - if only a little - at this apparent disregard for his still breathing wife who was probably suffering at home while he took Jean out for the day in his car[137].

Conan Doyle's view of golf was laid before the public in March. The *London Magazine* of that month carried an article in which a number of 'prominent and clever men' explained the allure of the game. *The Daily Mirror* of March 16th reported on this article.

Conan Doyle's love of the game was, according to the article, based on the fact that it 'can be played at all seasons, alone or in company'. He went on to confess 'I play it very badly but I know enough of it to appreciate its points.'

❧

March 27th saw Conan Doyle and his brother Innes involved in a car crash. The event took three days to reach the papers with the *Daily Express* covering the event in its issue of the 30th.

The article was entitled *Sir A. Conan Doyle's Narrow Escape.* It began by describing Conan Doyle as 'one of the most enthusiastic of motorists' and went on to describe how after returning to Undershaw from a 'spin with his brother' Conan Doyle had struck the gate of his home and overturned his car pinning both himself and Innes underneath it. Thanks to prompt assistance both men were left with nothing more than 'a few bruises'.

---

[137] Letter dated March 16th - *Arthur Conan Doyle: A Life in Letters* edited by Jon Lellenberg et al.

March also saw the completion of the Sherlock Holmes story *The Missing Three-Quarter*. This was the eleventh story in the new series and Conan Doyle must have been relieved that he was reaching the end. Unlike the majority of the other stories in the series, Conan Doyle did not specify the exact date of completion in his diary.

❧

On April 9th an important meeting was held in the schoolroom of the Hindhead Free Church. The meeting was to formally found the new Hindhead Golf Club.

In the autumn of 1903 tentative agreements had finally been put in place for the leasing of the land required for the new eighteen-hole course. Other enthusiastic golfers in the area had been working towards this since 1902.

Conan Doyle, although undoubtedly an interested party, did not attend the meeting which had two main purposes. The first was to formally found the club as an entity and secondly to elect the committee.

Possibly due to his absence from the meeting Conan Doyle was not elected to the committee at this stage. The positions of Chairman, Captain, Secretary and Treasurer were filled and the date for the first committee meeting was set for April 26th at the Royal Huts Hotel. Interestingly, amongst the elected committee members was a man by the name of A.L. Capon who owned the Moorlands Hotel in which Conan Doyle had stayed immediately prior to moving into Undershaw.

April also saw Conan Doyle conclude his commission for *Collier's Weekly* and *The Strand*. *The Abbey Grange* was completed and submitted.

Conan Doyle (left) and Innes Doyle in the Wolseley 6HP at Undershaw
(Courtesy of Georgina Doyle)

The Royal Huts Hotel, Hindhead c1900
(Author's collection)

Conan Doyle finished April by earning the ire of *The Daily Mirror*. They stated, in their issue of the 22nd, that he had referred to London as 'a city of mean streets'. They did not say where he had made the assertion but were quick to criticise him for it. Calling his remark 'absurd' they went on to say 'What about Piccadilly and Regent Street and Whitehall, three of the finest thoroughfares in Europe?' They concluded by saying 'If it were all like Shaftesbury Avenue or the Strand, Sir A. Conan Doyle's reproach might be justified. But even these are being gradually improved'.

In May Conan Doyle got round to honouring a forgotten commitment. He had promised a Sherlock Holmes story to *McClure's Magazine* and now decided that it was time to deliver it[138]. The recent series had been wrapped up quite neatly with *The Abbey Grange* and Conan Doyle had no desire to give people any idea that there was another series in the offing. The pressing problem therefore was how to create a story without giving people the wrong idea.

He decided to repeat the trick that he had employed for *The Hound of the Baskervilles*. He would write the story and make plain that its events had occurred many years previously. Presumably after trawling through his previous stories he alighted upon *The Second Stain* which had been mentioned by name in *The Naval Treaty* which had been published in 1893 just before *The Final Problem*.

The story opens with Watson making it plain that *The Abbey Grange* was supposed to be the last recorded exploit of Holmes. The reason for the additional story now being put

[138] *Conan Doyle: The Man Who Created Sherlock Holmes* by Andrew Lycett. *McClure's* had originally wanted a whole series but had agreed to settle for a longer than usual single story.

before the public was given as 'It was only upon my representing to him [Holmes] that I had given a promise that "The Adventure of the Second Stain" should be published when the times were ripe..'.

Watson's reasons therefore mirrored Conan Doyle's own - the story was published in order to honour a prior commitment. In his diary, Conan Doyle recorded that the story was ten thousand words long. With the exception of *The Adventure of the Priory School,* which had over eleven thousand words, all the stories published since 1903 had been around eight to nine thousand words in length. It seems reasonably clear that Conan Doyle made the story longer than average in an attempt to appease *McClure's* who had expressed a preference for an entire series. However, it seems that *McClure's* were not legally bound to accept the story. When the cost of securing it was put to them they decided to pass. Another likely reason for them choosing not to take the story was that they would be required to wait for *Collier's* to finish the stories they were still running before the most recent could be published.

As a result the story was offered to *Collier's* and *The Strand.* Both gratefully took it. Greenhough Smith was able to publish it in December. Hapgood had to hold onto the story until January 1905 as he was still running the four stories that preceded it.

❧

June 18th saw the second annual dinner of the Pilgrims' Society[139]. This was the society that existed to foster good relations between the United States and Great Britain. On this occasion the event was in honour of its President Lord Roberts and chaired by the U.S. Ambassador Joseph Hodges Choate.

---

[139] *The Times* of June 20th 1904.

Samuel McClure, founder of McClure's Magazine (1914)

Conan Doyle in his study (1904)
(Author's collection)

Conan Doyle's study viewed through the doorway. This picture was the frontispiece to his 1908 book Through the Magic Door
(Author's collection)

The dinner was held at the Savoy Hotel and, in honour of the president, the room was 'decorated in the style of an Indian tent'. The overwhelming majority of the guests were either political or military. Two of the noted names that did not fall into either category were those of Conan Doyle and Bertram Fletcher Robinson. The fact that both men attended the dinner could be taken as yet more evidence that there was no falling out over *The Hound of the Baskervilles* but as we don't know if they sat near each other or even spoke we cannot rely on it as evidence.

❧

It is easy to fall into the trap of assuming that Louise Conan Doyle barely left Undershaw during her years of residency. The image of the ailing wife holding her husband back is one that, thanks to some of the earliest biographical works, is hard to get away from. However she was far from idle as was demonstrated by an article in *The Daily Mirror* of September 15th.

The newspaper reported that Louise had been one of two judges in a competition held by the *Tatler* magazine to find the prettiest child in England. The winner had been a girl by the name of Queenie May Wells from Teddington. The newspaper, rather ungallantly, implied that it was not happy with the result by proposing to hold its own competition. They explicitly requested parents to send in pictures of their children if they believed them to be prettier than the *Tatler's* winner. They also implied that the original contest favoured girls by proposing that their competition would have separate divisions for boys and girls. This was because 'the standard of beauty would not apply equally to both'.

The Adventure of the One Statuette

September 22nd saw Conan Doyle in Southwark Police Court in response to a summons. The summons had been issued on behalf of William George Jones, his partner in the Sculptograph.

It seems reasonably clear that since the device had been mentioned the previous year there had been some falling out between the two men and the court summons was the latest episode.

According to the report in the *Daily Express* of September 23rd, the dispute revolved around a statuette entitled *A Girl at a Fountain* which had been lent to the Automatic Sculpture Company. The company was one in which Conan Doyle had an interest.

Jones took exception to this and issued a summons on Conan Doyle for the statuette's detention. The battle was subsequently fought out between the two men's solicitors. These were Mr. Newton for Jones and Mr. Abinger for Conan Doyle.

Newton opened by stating that his client now wished to withdraw the action on the grounds that the statuette had been returned since the summons was issued. All he wanted now was costs awarded against Conan Doyle.

Abinger pointed out that Jones had made no attempt to secure the statuette prior to issuing the summons and that he could have claimed it directly from the company holding it at any time he wished. This course of action had subsequently been pursued by Conan Doyle after he had made a telephone call to the company on September 10th to request its return.

In a sign of how bad relations had become Abinger stated that his client should be the one to be awarded costs and that it was his belief that Jones had pursued the action with the sole purpose of 'annoying his client'. In addition he stated that 'Sir Arthur was anxious to put a stop to the persistent annoyance from Mr. Jones' and that in this case it was his belief that the object of the action was concerned with 'getting money from Sir Arthur'.

According to *The Daily Mirror* of the same date (which covered the story under the heading *Annoyed Novelist*), Newton responded by saying 'I entirely deny the statements of my friend. They are absolutely without foundation.' To this Abinger said 'Well, we will see'.

The magistrate pointed out that it was not within his power to award costs to either side and that the parties would need to take the argument to another court. Ultimately all he could do was withdraw the summons[140].

The Daily Mirror of October 10th carried a short piece entitled *Last of Sherlock Holmes.* Conan Doyle had completed his story *The Adventure of the Second Stain* a few months earlier. The existence of the story was evidently no secret and as it was clearly separate from the earlier stories speculation was no doubt rife that more might follow.

---

[140] In Conan Doyle's diaries for 1905 and 1906 there are scattered entries regarding a sculpture. On occasion the entries are slightly more explicit and state 'sculpture meeting' along with a time. It is not clear whether or not these entries are related to the sculptograph but, if they are, it suggests that Conan Doyle took an active interest in it for some time.

The *Mirror*'s interviewer must have put a question to this effect to Conan Doyle who stated in response that this would be the last story of the great detective. He went on to say, displaying a large amount of wishful thinking, 'I am rather tired of Sherlock Holmes, and I suspect the public is too.'

In his writing Conan Doyle had so often had his art imitate real life. The *Daily Express* of October 27th listed a curious incident of life imitating *his* art. The article was entitled *Affluent Beggar* and concerned a man named Cecil de Smith, an electrical engineer who lived in Upper Norwood. He was well known in the City where, under the guise of a match seller, he was successfully begging and taking home approximately six pounds a week.

His day over, this supposedly paralysed man (one of his arms was completely limp) would then make his way to a tobacconist where he changed his many coins into notes before making his way to London Bridge station to catch a train home to Crystal Palace. Somehow, on the journey, he would alter his appearance and emerge a different man (with two working arms). A constable who followed him for a day described him as stepping off the train and heading straight for a bar where he ordered two dozen oysters. After this repast he made his way to a 'tryst with a young lady' before eventually heading home to his wife at their rented villa. The villa was described as costing thirty pounds a year to rent - something Smith would have earned in around five weeks. He was remanded at the Guildhall Police Court.

The similarities to Conan Doyle's story *The Man with the Twisted Lip* (1891) are surely beyond coincidence and make you wonder if anyone else had attempted to emulate Conan Doyle's stories to their own advantage.

❧

December 6th saw the publication in *The Strand* of *The Adventure of the Second Stain.* Advertisements appeared throughout the press to mark the event. The advertisement in *The Daily Mirror* of that date stated 'Few indeed will not regret to hear that "The Adventure of the Second Stain," by SIR A. CONAN DOYLE, will be the last "Sherlock Holmes" story that talented author will ever write.'

Of course it was ultimately not the last but it was the last to be penned at Undershaw.

1905

Mr President

In the early days of 1905 the committee of the new Hindhead Golf Club, at its annual general meeting, offered Conan Doyle the position of president. This was a new position, or at least one that had not yet been occupied even if it had been created at the first committee meeting. Needless to say Conan Doyle accepted.

The presidency was the first of two honours he accepted in the early months of the year. The *Daily Mirror* of April 8th reported that the previous day Conan Doyle had been made an honorary doctor of laws by his alma mater Edinburgh University. Unlike certain earlier honours this was one he was positively pleased to accept. He even wrote to his mother on the subject describing it as an occasion where he would get 'capped'. The award clearly put him into a good mood and this was just as well as the golf club of which he was now the head was not enjoying an easy birth.

Of the required eighteen holes only seven were ready (and then only for practice) and money was running out. Things became so bad that on April 28th a committee meeting was called at which finances were a central item on the agenda. Precisely what actions were agreed upon is not known but as little as two weeks later Conan Doyle found himself one amongst several members offering emergency loans to keep the club afloat. In Conan Doyle's case the amount was one hundred pounds.

At around the same time the club gained a new member whose presence was to prove decidedly divisive. His name was

Alfred H. Wood and he was Conan Doyle's secretary. It is highly likely that, as both his friend and employer, Conan Doyle proposed Wood's membership. The club committee did not raise any objection but certain members probably wished that they had in later years. A mere two months after his membership had been approved, Wood, on the recommendation of club captain Whitaker, was elected to the committee. Once in position Wood slowly began to take over the club and did so, presumably, with Conan Doyle's blessing.

His ascent began with him chairing some meetings and continued when he was placed in charge of setting the handicaps of club members. If any members of the club had concerns at his rapid rise they said nothing.

On May 4th the *Daily Express* carried a small article announcing the publication of some new detective stories. The stories in question were collected under the heading of *The Chronicles of Addington Peace*[141]. The author was the newspaper's recently departed employee Bertram Fletcher Robinson who was now editor of *Vanity Fair*.

The article mentioned Robinson's connection to Conan Doyle through *The Hound of the Baskervilles.* This was clearly done as a means of assuring potential buyers that the stories were of a good standard. In turn, this could be taken as another argument against the oft repeated claim of a falling out between the two men in the aftermath of the publication of Conan Doyle's story. If the two men had fallen out as badly as some have claimed it would hardly be likely that Conan Doyle would have permitted newspapers to use his story as a way of

[141] The article named the publishers as Harper and Brothers and the price as three shillings and six pence. They had first been published as separate stories in *The Lady's Home Magazine of Fiction* the previous year.

effectively endorsing the work of a man he no longer wished to associate with. It is also likely, given what is known of Robinson's character, that he would have objected to being seen to trade on the name of someone he was not on good terms with.

On May 5th Conan Doyle was at Mansion House in London for the farewell dinner in honour of the outgoing U.S. Ambassador to Britain, Joseph Hodges Choate.

Joseph Hodges Choate - US Ambassador to Britain 1899 - 1905
(Pictured in 1910)

The event was covered in the following day's issue of the *Daily Express*. Besides Conan Doyle and fellow author Rudyard Kipling the names listed belonged almost exclusively to the world of politics and Conan Doyle did not participate in any of the speech making. Choate, in his speech, expressed much fondness for his period in the country and remarked favourably that a war between the nations was, in his view, simply not possible. 'We have got along without it for the last ninety years, and we shall get along perfectly well without it for the next 900 years,' he said.

On May 20th Conan Doyle was driving on the Portsmouth Road through the village of Shalford. He was stopped by an Inspector Jennings who had calculated his speed at thirty miles an hour. As the speed limit in force was twenty miles per hour Conan Doyle was charged with speeding.

The case came to court in Guildford on Saturday June 3rd[142]. Sir William Chance, a Cambridge graduate and barrister, chaired the session. Conan Doyle's defence was weak. He said that he did not believe his car was capable of such speed and that he had tried to exceed twenty miles per hour on several occasions and had failed. Although the newspaper coverage did not go into detail, one hopes that Conan Doyle emphasised that his attempts to exceed twenty miles per hour had been confined to areas where it was legal to do so. His counsel, Mr Owtram, attempted to elicit leniency by suggesting that it was difficult for a motorist to correctly judge his speed when heading downhill.

This argument did not satisfy Chance who clearly did not believe that a speed difference of ten miles per hour was imperceptible. Conan Doyle was fined five pounds.

---

[142] According to *The Times* of June 5th.

Given the chronological information that we have it seems likely that this journey was one made between Hindhead and London as Conan Doyle appeared only two days later at the Hotel Cecil for the centenary dinner of the Royal Medical and Chirurgical Society of London.

The *Daily Express* of May 27th carried an interesting entry under its column entitled *World's Happenings*. It reported that a special commission had elected to exclude *The Return of Sherlock Holmes* from all school libraries in Minnesota. The article reported that 'it' (presumably Minnesota as a whole) 'is said to savour too much of "Old Sleuth"'.

June 23rd saw Conan Doyle as part of the assembly welcoming the new U.S. Ambassador to Britain - Whitelaw Reid.

This welcome took the form of a dinner at Claridge's Hotel which was hosted by the Pilgrims' Society and consequently contained a much wider range of guests. In fact it was, according to the *Daily Express* of the 24th, a more art and literature driven guest list. Alongside the many politicians were the likes of Henry Irving, Rudyard Kipling, H. Rider Haggard and Lord Tennyson.[143]

After speeches by Lord Roberts, the society president, and Arthur Balfour, the Prime Minister, the new ambassador got to his feet. To great applause he echoed very much the spirit of cooperation proposed by his predecessor. For the 'two great branches of the English-speaking family' to not cooperate would, he said, be 'unnatural, difficult, against instinct and monstrous'.

The evening concluded with poetry which was read out by Irving.

---

[143] This was not the famous poet but his son Hallam, the second Baron Tennyson and former Governor-General of Australia, a position he had left only the previous year.

Whitelaw Reid - U.S. Ambassador to Britain 1905 - 1912

❧

August saw the fourth annual general meeting of Raphael Tuck & Sons. Conan Doyle was able to announce to the assembled company that the firm had successfully been the first to bring quality colour printing to Britain. Furthermore he was able to announce that 'oilettes' (the highest quality colour prints) were almost exclusively produced in Britain by the firm[144].

It was also a great source of pride to Conan Doyle that retailers of colour prints in Germany, the leader in quality colour printing, were importing prints from Britain to sell in their own shops. He concluded by stating 'I think, considering how long the current has been setting the other way, it is very pleasant to think that, by our exertions, we have turned it, and that we are making British art more appreciated on the Continent than it has been up till now.'

❧

The Penny Illustrated Paper and Illustrated Times of August 26th reported the marriage on August 16th of actress Decima Moore to Major Frederick Gordon Guggisberg. For both parties it was their second marriage.

Conan Doyle had a connection to both bride and groom. He knew the bride as she had played the part of Babs in *Jane Annie* in 1893. This was the ill-fated play on which he had collaborated with J.M. Barrie. It had met with decidedly mixed reviews and was widely considered a failure[145].

Guggisberg was a personal friend although it is not clear exactly how long they had known each other. Guggisberg first appeared in the Undershaw visitor book in August 1903 and it

---

[144] *The Penny Illustrated Paper and Illustrated Times* of August 5th.

[145] More about *Jane Annie* can be found in *The Norwood Author* by your present author.

is possible that the men had first come to each other's attention in 1901 when they both had books published that concerned military matters.

Guggisberg had visited Undershaw again in August 1904. The purpose of his visit on each occasion is unknown but it is possible that the second visit concerned his divorce from his first wife or his forthcoming marriage to Moore. If the latter, it is perfectly possible that it was on this occasion that he asked Conan Doyle to be his best man. Even if it was not, Conan Doyle did agree to fulfil the role[146].

Given that Conan Doyle agreed to serve as best man it is clear that he was on good terms with the couple; however his goodwill towards the new Mrs Guggisberg may have been sorely tested in later years when she became active in the suffragette movement. Conan Doyle was appalled by what he saw as their unwarranted levels of violence.

The same edition of the newspaper carried an article entitled *"Sherlock Holmes" in Court*. It detailed how, during the previous week, Conan Doyle had been in the city of Liverpool gathering 'local colour'. During the course of his visit he saw over the police buildings in the company of the chief constable and made his way up from the police cells and into the courtroom itself. This was a cause of some surprise to the magistrate, a Mr Stewart, who was present and had only recently concluded the day's proceedings.

---

[146] On each of his visits Guggisberg's name in the visitor book was followed by that of an Alfred Carpenter. Carpenter was a member of the Royal Navy who in 1901 was an Able Seaman on the HMS St George. The fact that both men attended together on both occasions suggests that Carpenter may have been some kind of aide to Guggisberg.

Decima Moore starring as Alice Coverdale in My Lady Molly at the Lyceum Theatre (1903)

The most curious aspect of the report was its assertion that the purpose of Conan Doyle's visit was that he was 'gathering material for a new series of Sherlock Holmes stories'. Furthermore the paper stated that these stories would focus especially on bank frauds. Given that Conan Doyle's next Sherlock Holmes story was almost exactly three years away; it is interesting to wonder where the paper got its information from[147].

Conan Doyle's most likely reason for being in Liverpool would have been to visit his brother. Innes had taken command of number six depot RFA (Royal Field Artillery) in Seaforth in December of 1904[148]. Seaforth was only about five miles north of Liverpool and it appears that Conan Doyle stopped by on more than one occasion to join in with Innes' social whirl[149].

The subject of motoring and, more specifically, speeding reared its head towards the end of September. The *Daily Mail* of September 21st carried a letter from Conan Doyle entitled *More Motorphobia*. In it he suggested that the police and magistrates of the country were targeting motorists as an easy way of raising money[150].

He drew particular attention to Guildford where he noted that the number of arrests and convictions for speeding were exactly the same which he thought was suspicious. His reasoning was that it was not possible for the police to be one hundred percent certain of a motorist's speed in every single case and that therefore the number of convictions should be less than the number of arrests.

---

147 The Sherlock Holmes story in question was *The Singular Experience of Mr J. Scott Eccles*. This was published in *Collier's Weekly* in August 1908. It would later be merged with its second part *The Tiger of San Pedro* and be seen in books as *The Adventure of Wisteria Lodge* which formed part of the collection *His Last Bow*. This would be published in book form in October 1917.

148 Many thanks to Georgina Doyle for this information.

149 The single entry 'Liverpool' appears in his diary for October 10th 1905.

150 *Letters to the Press* edited by John Gibson and Richard Lancelyn Green.

He also counselled readers to be especially careful in Folkestone. He had been fined ten pounds and nine shillings there on September 1st for speeding. He warned readers that the police of the area were in the habit of lying in wait within churchyards, which he viewed as sacrilege and thus a greater crime than speeding.

Revival

Late September saw William Gillette return to London and the Duke of York's Theatre with his play *Clarice*. As a curtain raiser to this play he decided to also put on a one-act Holmes play that he had penned and played earlier that year in New York.

The piece, entitled *The Painful Predicament of Sherlock Holmes*, saw Gillette partnered for the first time with the young Charles Chaplin as Billy the pageboy. Chaplin had begun playing the role of Billy in the original *Sherlock Holmes* play in 1903 when it was touring the country in the aftermath of its Lyceum run. Chaplin had longed to play in a significant West End theatre and to play alongside an actor as famous as Gillette must have been seen by him as a significant honour.

However it looked as though Chaplin's West End engagement was destined to be short. *Clarice* was a flop and closed, in October, after a mere thirteen performances. Gillette, in order to rescue the season, opened on the 17th with a revival of *Sherlock Holmes*. After six years the play returned to the site of its first ever performance and Chaplin, no doubt to his immense relief, was retained for the role of Billy[151].

The Penny Illustrated Paper and Illustrated Times of October 28th reported on William Gillette's revival of his famous play and viewed it as an 'unqualified success'. Special mention was made of the scenes between Holmes and Moriarty

---

[151] *Sherlock Holmes Journal (Winter 1967 Volume 8 Number 3)*

and the effect that the play continued to have on the audience after so many years.

In November *The New York Times* of the 19th carried an article entitled *Conan Doyle's Hard Luck as a Playwright.* It concerned his attempts to get his latest play, an adaptation of *Brigadier Gerard*, onto the stage.

The interview, which took place at Undershaw, did not however confine itself to this new play. The interviewer naturally got round to the subject of Sherlock Holmes and the Gillette play. Conan Doyle said that the Holmes play was 'almost entirely by Mr. William Gillette. He took my story and used it, as it seemed to him, to the best effect.'

He then mentioned that he would be writing a prequel to *The White Company*[152]. After confirming that it was his favourite work he announced that its prequel or, as he called it, 'a prelude' would be called *Sir Nigel* after one of *The White Company*'s notable characters. He also stated, perhaps overconfidently, that the idea of writing a prequel was almost unique stating 'to write two novels in this way is one which I have never heard of anybody else adopting.'

The interviewer presumably asked for the reason for this approach. To this Conan Doyle answered:

> 'Why am I going back this way? Because I am tired of "Sherlock Holmes", I want to do some more solid work again. "Sherlock" and "Gerard" are alright in their own way, but, after all, one gets very little satisfaction from such work afterwards.'

Conan Doyle went on to announce that he was not likely to write *any* short stories for some time but conceded that he

---

[152] By October 6th 1905, according to the *Daily Mirror* of that date, Conan Doyle had in fact written three-quarters of the book.

would take the advice of his editors (and presumably - publishers).

In the same month Conan Doyle wrote to Greenhough Smith regarding *Sir Nigel* which was to commence serialisation in December. Even though he personally had made it clear that the book's events preceded those in *The White Company* he decided that he did not wish *The Strand* to mention this.

'I think the allusion to the White Company is better omitted' he stated. His concern was, given the time elapsed since the publication of *The White Company*, that people who had not read his earlier work might be put off from reading his latest. In his letter to Smith he stated that he believed that the average reader, if told about *The White Company*, would fail to understand that his new story could be read in isolation.[153]

For his part it seems that Smith had expressed reservations about the book's title to which Conan Doyle had responded by saying that the title was perfectly fine and that 'we will stick to it'.

The year came to a melancholy close in December with the death of Conan Doyle's mother-in-law Emily Hawkins. She was buried in Reigate and her funeral made the front page of the *Daily Express* of the 29th. Its prominence was nothing to do with her or indeed her famous son-in-law. It made the front page thanks to the novelty of a 'motor-car as a hearse'.

It is no exaggeration to say that Mrs Hawkins and her daughter had been very close and the loss hit Louise hard. It is perhaps too much to say that it made her health worse but it certainly did not help matters.

Conan Doyle also owed his mother-in-law a debt. It was her willingness to look after her grandchildren at short-notice that had allowed him to take his wife to Europe in 1891 when he wanted to catch up on the latest advances in ophthalmic medicine and again in 1893 when he had taken Louise to Switzerland in the battle to improve her health.

---

[153] Letter held at the British Library.

1906

Golfing Troubles and Bereavement

The General Election dominated January 1906. Back in September 1902 rumours had circulated to the effect that Conan Doyle had designs of fighting the Scottish seat of Hawick Burghs. Journalists at the *Daily Express* had sought confirmation of this and sent a telegram to Undershaw. They reported, in their issue of September 29th 1902, that they had received the curt response 'No - Doyle'.

In a letter dated November 19th 1902 Conan Doyle had gone on to state that he did not see himself as a party man but could see himself standing in the future as an independent[154].

Over time he shifted from both positions. *The Daily Mirror* of November 14th 1903 reported that he had consented to be the Liberal Unionist candidate for the Scottish seat and, in December, the same newspaper briefly reported a speech made by Conan Doyle in Hawick on the subject of commerce and free trade[155]. The *Daily Express* of June 7th 1904 showed that Conan Doyle was putting a lot of energy into politics when it reported that 'Sir A. Conan Doyle is arranging for an election tour in Scotland.' They also pointed out that he intended to tour 'disguised as a cricketer.'

Despite this long and confusing preamble he was now fighting the Scottish seat on behalf of the Liberal Unionists. His

---

[154] Letter held at British Library.

[155] The article on November 14th 1903 also reported that, on that visit, Conan Doyle had donated £1000 to Edinburgh University for the purposes of founding a scholarship for South African students.

opponent, Thomas Shaw - the Lord Advocate, had held the seat since 1892 for the Liberal Party but at the most recent election, in 1900, his majority was less than three hundred. Despite the fact that the Liberals had held the seat since its creation the Liberal Unionists clearly felt it was for the taking.

This belief no doubt had its basis in the issue of Tariff Reform. The wool industry in the region was being badly hit by cheap imports and Conan Doyle was very much in favour of imposing taxation on such imports to make it easier for British companies to compete inside their own borders[156]. In 1903 he had even gone so far as to collect a number of his speeches on the subject into a book entitled *Tariff Reform - With special reference to the Scottish Woollen Industry.* His position had made him a natural ally of the prominent Liberal Unionist M.P. Joseph Chamberlain who felt the same as he did and the two men exchanged correspondence on this and other issues.

As with the election in 1900, Conan Doyle sent a letter to a local newspaper (*The Border Telegraph* of Galashiels) in which he stated his electoral position. The letter was published by the paper in their issue of January 9th which was nine days before polling day.

Despite this and his other political activities, Conan Doyle's campaign did not appeal to the local electorate. The *Daily Express* of January 18th reported him to be amongst the defeated candidates. For Shaw it was a resounding success with his majority increasing to nearly seven hundred. Perhaps it was the fact that he had actually increased the majority of his opponent that finally caused Conan Doyle to abandon the idea of ever sitting in Parliament[157].

There were a number of people who were upset at Conan Doyle's defeat. A family who lived in Galashiels felt moved to express their sorrow in a letter which was signed by the entire

---

[156] He had declared his support for Tariff Reform in a letter dated July 4th 1903 which had appeared in *The Spectator*.

[157] Conan Doyle's election leaflet which set out what he stood for was printed and published by Raphael Tuck & Sons.

household. In addition to the fairly predictable expressions of consolation the letter's author added an interesting postscript.

P.S. If the ladies had had but votes I am sure you would have got in by a huge majority[158].

This sentence must have hit home a little given that Conan Doyle was an opponent of women's suffrage.

He also received a similar letter of condolence from the Hawick Parish Church in which the parish priest remarked 'how deeply sorry I am that you are lost to us'.

The most notable words of consolation came from Joseph Chamberlain. He sent a telegram to Undershaw on January 18th in which he stated 'Very much regret your defeat after a splendid fight.'

However when the telegram arrived Conan Doyle was not at home. A member of the household arranged for Chamberlain's message to be forwarded and a second telegram bearing his message arrived for Conan Doyle at the Grand Hotel in London the next day[159].

Sadly 1906 saw not only the death of Conan Doyle's political ambitions but also those of Chamberlain himself. In the middle of the year he suffered a severe stroke which effectively ended his hopes of achieving the highest office although after his recovery he did remain an M.P. for some years.

Back at Hindhead events were equally rocky and began with the annual general meeting of the Golf Club. The meeting marked the beginning of the end for Alfred Wood's membership although it probably did not seem like it at the time. Wood, who already chaired some meetings and controlled club handicapping, was elected to the position of club treasurer.

Given the club's less than ideal financial state it is possible that he was elected to the post by some members who resented

[158] From the letter held at the British Library.
[159] The British Library holds both telegrams.

his power and wanted to see him fail. If Wood had any qualms over the challenges of the position it is clear he was not put off from accepting it.

Joseph Chamberlain (1836 - 1914)

The task ahead of him was not an enviable one. Despite having been officially founded almost two years previously the club was not yet formally open and it was surviving on loans from existing members and from admitting new members despite the inability for them to do little more than practice on the holes that were complete[160].

Wood's fall from grace began in April when he was forced to report, at a committee meeting, that the club was ninety-eight pounds overdrawn with outstanding bills totalling over one hundred pounds.

The reaction to this can only be described as one of panic. The committee promptly fired several grounds workers to save money and again turned to wealthy backers for assistance. Conan Doyle once again dug deep and offered a gift of fifty pounds combined with a further loan of one hundred pounds. This brought his total contributions to date to three hundred and fifty pounds[161].

Upon receipt of this, and presumably other, money the hastily sacked employees were promptly re-employed, which must have been confusing and stressful for them, and work on the course resumed.

The reason for the committee's panic has to be looked at. Their reaction to Wood's dire financial report suggests that they had little or no idea of the scale of the problems the club was facing. Did Wood's predecessor as treasurer keep the dire situation from them or did the situation only become perilous after Wood had taken over the position?

Anyone wishing Wood's removal from the post was placed into a dilemma. He was Conan Doyle's friend, had his ear and was probably the only person capable of securing the gifts and loans the club was receiving. It is likely that no one at any level in the club desired to take on its famous president and risk the loans being called in.

It was certainly the case that all was not well between the committee members. Wood's dominance of meetings continued and the relationship between him and Whitaker had deteriorated

---

[160] In *Out of the Shadows* Georgina Doyle tells us that Conan Doyle and many others continued to play at Hankley while the new club was being prepared.

[161] Akin to twenty thousand pounds in today's money.

to such an extent that the captain was frequently absent from meetings which Wood attended.

The only committee member successfully navigating this minefield of personalities was the long-suffering secretary Edward Turle. Turle was not only the club's secretary but also the owner and schoolmaster of Hindhead School where Conan Doyle's son Kinglsey had been a pupil until 1903 when he had become a boarder at Sandroyd School.

Turle clearly loved both the school and the club but was starting to feel more drawn to the game of golf and perhaps also felt that the club's shaky foundations needed more attention. In order to provide this attention he made the decision to sell the school and devote himself full-time to the demands of the golf club. This not only meant giving up the school but also moving home as he was living on the school premises. He successfully sold the school before the end of the year and officially became a full-time club member.

Returning to March, *The New York Times* of March 3rd carried a report of an interview with Conan Doyle that had clearly taken place at least a day earlier as it mentioned that he was busy attending rehearsals of his play *Brigadier Gerard* which was due to debut at the Imperial Theatre that very day. Whatever problems Conan Doyle had been experiencing a few months earlier getting his plays taken on had clearly been overcome.

In the interview Conan Doyle stated that he would never take an author's call no matter how flattering it might be. He also made it clear that he considered a playwright to be a braver soul than a novelist stating 'the man who writes a novel does not bring down a whole company with him if the public won't have his work.'

He also emphasised that his latest play was his 'first whole-evening play.' By this, of course, he meant that *Sherlock*

Holmes and *Jane Annie* had been, to varying extents, collaborations and that *Waterloo* had only been a curtain raiser.

Although he was clearly quite excited about the debut of his new play it was not going out quite as he had originally envisaged. He had expressed the hope in his November interview that the actor Martin Harvey would play the title role of Gerard. He had presumably seen Harvey act at the Lyceum where he had been part of Henry Irving's company and had played numerous minor roles.

Martin Harvey (date unknown)

However Harvey was unavailable for the role as he was committed to the part of Brian O'Carroll in the play *Boy O'Carroll* which was due to open in the Theatre Royal, Newcastle in April[162]. Ultimately actor Lewis Waller agreed to take on the play. Conan Doyle had learned of this news on his return from Scotland and referred to it as 'the first bit of luck I have had for some time'. Whereas Harvey had been part of Irving's company, Waller had risen to prominence under Herbert Beerbohm Tree.

The Penny Illustrated Paper and Illustrated Times of March 3rd reminded its readers that the play's first performance was due that evening. The article, however, had clearly been written the previous day as it described the play as taking place 'tomorrow (Saturday) evening'.

The issue of the same paper which appeared the following Saturday (March 10th) carried a review of the debut performance. It was rather ambivalent in its tone and began by stating that Conan Doyle was clearly 'not as expert a dramatist as he is a novelist'.

The first act was praised as 'admirable' but that afterwards the play 'steadily deteriorates'. Despite this, Lewis Waller came in for consistent praise as did many of his fellow principals. The review concluded that 'the play was very well received, and should have a successful career'[163].

The *Daily Express* of the 7th covered the performance in its regular column *Green Room Gossip*. They had the advantage of actually speaking to Conan Doyle and getting his reaction to some of the criticism.

---

[162] Harvey's play moved to the Imperial Theatre on May 19th 1906. Presumably this was after *Brigadier Gerard* finished its run.

[163] The play ultimately ran for 114 performances at the Imperial Theatre. Lewis Waller went on to play Gerard again in the silent film *Brigadier Gerard* which was released in the same year as his death (1915).

Lewis Waller (1860 - 1915)
(Author's collection)

Conan Doyle was described as 'delighted with the public reception'. He recounted how the play had been offered to 'about ten managers, who all refused it'. He was very clearly indulging in a little show of *I told you so* to those managers. As if to labour the point he reminded the reporter how his novel *Micah Clarke* had been refused by almost a dozen publishers but had gone on to be well received.

With regards to the members of the press who had looked upon the play unfavourably, Conan Doyle was of the opinion that they had collectively become 'jaded' and much more likely to be inflexible 'sticklers for conventionalities'. He saw this in stark contrast to the layman who was more inclined to trust the author's judgement.

He also firmly made the point that the humour or 'comicality', as it was described, was entirely intentional and that the audience had been laughing where he intended them to laugh - a point which had apparently been lost on some critics who had failed to see that the humour was intentional.

The article closed with the reporter stating that Conan Doyle was happy and bore no malice towards his critics. Had the play not been a success one wonders if he would have been so obliging.

His positive attitude received an additional boost from the mam who wrote to him about the play on March 12th, presumably in response to a letter from her son voicing his concerns. As usual she gave him the shot in the arm that he needed telling him that the play would do well and that he should not concern himself with the opinion of the critics.

The Daily Mirror editions of March 19th and 21st carried details of a crime committed against Conan Doyle. The issue on the 19th, under the heading *Last Night's News Items*, mentioned that two men had appeared at 'Worship Street' on Saturday 17th in connection with the theft of package[164].

The package contained, amongst other things, some family photographs. The newspaper gave remarkably inaccurate details of two of them which were, according to them 'Photographs of "Louis [sic] Conan Doyle and Mary Conan Doyle," said to be the mother and sister of Sir Arthur Conan Doyle'.

Details emerged in the later issue to the effect that a man by the name of William Payne had stolen the package from a Pickford's removal van. Payne was sentenced to three months' hard labour on the 20th. The fate of the other man supposedly involved in the theft was not detailed.

The burning questions of course were where the theft took place, why Conan Doyle was moving packages with Pickford's and where the destination was[165].

April saw Conan Doyle remind the country once again of his belief in the usefulness of rifle ranges. The *Daily Express* of the 14th reported on a visit a reporter had made to Undershaw two days previously. The reporter remarked that upon arriving at the house he had found Conan Doyle 'stretched on the turf leisurely making bull's-eyes and "magpies[166]"' while his daughter Mary marked down the score from behind a bullet-proof screen. Conan Doyle was not happy with what he clearly saw as the lack of established rifle clubs and this was a way of bringing the subject back before the public at large.

Conan Doyle was also having problems with his own club. At some point the decision had been made to allow the

---

164 The newspaper's reference to Worship Street was inaccurate. The Old Street Magistrates Court which had once been on that site had, in 1906, been moved to nearby Old Street which, given its name, was more appropriate.

165 At the time of writing the author does not know the answers to these questions.

166 Magpies are hits just outside of the bulls-eye.

Undershaw club to operate on Sundays. This was a step too far for some of the more pious members of Hindhead who evidently began to complain. Some of these complaints made their way into the local press and Conan Doyle chose to answer them through the same medium. The chosen newspaper was *The Farnham, Haslemere & Hindhead Herald*. In their issue of April 28th, Conan Doyle pointed out that he and the club committee had anticipated the opposition and that no shooting went on during the hours of the church services. He also made it plain that he had no intention of stopping practice on Sundays. As a final point he drew attention to the fact that in days gone by (he highlighted the reign of James I) shooting on Sundays had been almost compulsory.

A few weeks later *The Penny Illustrated Paper and Illustrated Times* of May 5th carried a picture of Kingsley taking aim on the same range under the supervision of Alfred Wood and other members of the rifle club.

May 24th saw Conan Doyle once again dining at the Hotel Cecil. On this occasion the meal was in honour of Lord Milner, the former High Commissioner for Southern Africa. In an impressive display of organisation the dinner had been arranged for over five hundred guests in just six weeks. It was a commendably apolitical event with members of all parties present. However Conan Doyle was very much the lone author as the overwhelming majority of the guests were political or military.

Four days later Louise Conan Doyle had what was probably the last social evening of her life. In the company of Innes she went to the Imperial Theatre to see her husband's new play performed and met Lewis Waller at its conclusion. Innes was close to his sister-in-law and arguably had considerably more time for her than his brother did. Little did either of them know that it would be the last time that they would see each other[167].

Lord Milner (First Viscount Milner)

[167] *Out of the Shadows* by Georgina Doyle.

On June 30th the long awaited official opening of Hindhead Golf Club finally took place. *The Times* covered the event in their issue of July 2nd.

The main event was an exhibition match between two of the most famous golfers of the day - James Braid and John Henry Taylor.

James Braid (1913)

John Henry Taylor (c1910)

Both men were winners of the British Open Golf Championship. James Braid was the champion that year[168]. The match was played over thirty-six holes and, at the end of the morning, with the first eighteen holes completed, Braid had a lead of six holes. In the afternoon Taylor clawed back a few holes but the match still went to Braid who was clearly on better form.

The Times had a generally favourable opinion of the course describing it as a 'thorough test of golf'. Beyond this and other brief comments about the course the article mentioned virtually nothing else about the event[169].

❧

Four days after the club's opening came the long-expected death of Louise Conan Doyle. About two weeks earlier specialists had visited Undershaw and had determined the end to be near and Conan Doyle had written letters to his mother and Innes detailing Louise's worsening condition. His letter to his brother referred to paralysis that Louise was suffering down her left side and also mentioned that there was evidence of some damage to her brain. In an attempt to make her last days as peaceful as possible the rifle range was closed and the miniature railway in the grounds was kept out of action[170].

---

[168] Both men won the Open five times. The advent of the First World War appears to have brought an end to both their careers.

[169] Conan Doyle's diary for 1906 almost suggests that the event was not seen as important by him. The entry for June 30th simply reads 'Hindhead Golf Club'.

[170] *Hindhead's Turn Will Come* by Ralph Irwin-Brown. Mention of the miniature railway first appeared in *The Life of Sir Arthur Conan Doyle* by John Dickson Carr. According to *The Adventures of Conan Doyle* by Charles Higham, William Gillette had admired the railway on his earlier visit to Undershaw and it inspired him to construct one at his own home.

Given the gloomy prognosis at the time her tuberculosis was diagnosed in October 1893 the fact that Louise had lived a further thirteen years was nothing short of miraculous. Even though Conan Doyle had tactlessly conducted a relationship, albeit platonic, with Jean Leckie under her nose for almost ten years (and deluded himself that it had gone unnoticed) her life had unquestionably been extended almost entirely by her husband's considerable efforts. His decision to move from favourable climate to favourable climate, regardless of where that climate was to be found, had enabled her to live far longer than had been believed possible and, just as importantly, allowed her to be a part of her children's lives almost into adulthood[171]. Therefore as tempting as it is to criticise Conan Doyle for his conduct with Jean he deserves praise in at least equal measure for extending his wife's life.

Sadly Louise's death went largely unreported in the press whose lack of interest in her in some ways mirrored the declining interest Conan Doyle himself had shown as his relationship with Jean Leckie went from strength to strength. Newspapers such as *The Daily News, The Era* and *The Graphic* did not appear to cover it. It seems that the only British newspapers to give Louise's death any space were *The Times,* the *Daily Mirror* and the *Daily Express*. The first stated, in their July 5th issue:

> LADY DOYLE, wife of Sir Arthur Conan Doyle, died at 3 o'clock yesterday morning at her residence, Undershaw, Hindhead. Lady Doyle, who was 49 years of age, had been in delicate health some years. She was the youngest daughter of Mr J. Hawkins, of Minsterworth, Gloucester, and married in 1886 Sir Arthur, then Dr., Conan Doyle and in medical practice at Southsea.

The *Daily Mirror's* report was largely the same as *The Times* and the *Daily Express* confined itself to one line albeit on

[171] At the time of Louise's death her daughter Mary was seventeen and her son Kingsley was thirteen (he turned fourteen in November).

the front page. On the same day as *The Times* and under the heading *Death of Lady Conan Doyle*, they stated 'Lady Conan Doyle, wife of Sir Arthur Conan Doyle, the novelist, died at Hindhead yesterday morning'.

The New York Times of the same date carried very much the same information as *The Times* under the heading 'Sir Conan Doyle's Wife Dead.' Her estate was later valued at four hundred and fifty-four pounds and the administration of this was later awarded to Conan Doyle[172].

The funeral was held at St Luke's Church in Grayshott. In addition to Conan Doyle the mourners included Innes, Willie Hornung, Alfred Wood and Edward Turle. An additional sign of how well regarded Louise had been came in the form of a floral tribute from the Undershaw servants.

Just under a month after Louise's death Conan Doyle spent some time at the Ashdown Park Hotel. Presumably his main purpose was to be close to Jean without causing any tongues to wag. He arrived on August 3rd and stayed for at least a week during which he took Innes (who joined him on the 10th) to dinner at the home of the Leckies[173]. While there he decided to contribute to a series of letters that had been running in the *Daily Express*. The newspaper had posed the question 'are we becoming less religious?' and Conan Doyle was not happy with the opinions expressed by many of those who had chosen to submit their thoughts.

In particular he took issue with those correspondents who suggested that the best measure of piety was attendance at church. His letter, which appeared in the August 7th issue, opened thus:

'It appears to me that one fallacy runs through a great deal of the correspondence about religion in your columns, and that is the postulate that any form of ritual, including the ritual of going to a

---

[172] This was reported in *The Times* of April 9th 1907. In the article Louise was referred to as Dame Louisa Doyle of Hindhead.
[173] *Out of the Shadows* by Georgina Doyle.

large stone building for the purpose of communion with the great unseen, has any bearing upon true religion.'

His argument against church attendance as a sign of religious fervour continued with 'Never yet have I known a person who was good because he went to church or evil because he did not.' It was not so much a tirade against religion as a tirade against religious observance being used as a sign of goodness.

He went on to provide a more practical set of criteria whereby the goodness of the human race might be judged:

(1) Is there a kinder and broader view of such subjects, enabling all men of all creeds to live in amity and charity?

(2) Are the criminal statistics better?

(3)Are the drink returns better, showing that man is acquiring greater animal self-control?

(4) Are the illegitimacy returns better, showing the same thing?

(5) Is there more reading, more demand for lectures, more interest in science, showing that the mind is gaining upon the body?

(6) Are the savings bank returns better, showing thrift and self-denial?

(7) Are the trade returns better, showing greater industry and efficiency?

(8) Are there more charitable institutions and does man show more clearly his sense of duty towards the lower animals?'

The grave, in St. Luke's Churchyard, Grayshott, of Louise Conan Doyle. The grave that can just be seen to the right is that for her children Mary and Kingsley
(Author's collection)

Conan Doyle's thoughts did not go unchallenged with subsequent writers taking issue with what some of them clearly saw as a thinly veiled attack on Christianity.

It is tempting to speculate as to Conan Doyle's reasons for contributing to this debate. Was it the result of pent up frustration over the objections to his rifle range operating on Sundays or was it something to do with Louise's death? In the aftermath of her funeral he must have reflected a lot on their life together and his attitude towards her as his interest in Jean Leckie had increased. Did he take the earlier suggestion that church attendance was an indicator of goodness personally? Did he subconsciously resent the suggestion that, as a non-churchgoer, he was in some way not a good man? Or was it purely and simply the case that he would have made the same contribution under any circumstances?

An interesting article appeared in the September 26th issue of the *Daily Mirror*, entitled *The Diamond Hunt* it explained that a British ship sailing on behalf of the Collis Diamond Syndicate had been prevented from putting its crew ashore on 'a mysterious island off the Cape coast'. Conan Doyle was amongst the shareholders of the expedition, another name was that of composer Sir Edward Elgar.

September also saw Kingsley commence his studies at Eton. One can only imagine how hard this must have been for him only two months after the loss of his mother.

The Scapegoat and the Umpire

It was towards the end of 1906 when Conan Doyle read an article that had appeared in the magazine *Umpire*. He later referred to his seeing this article as chance but it was nothing of the kind. The information had been sent to him by the piece's subject - a man by the name of George Edalji.

George Edalji

Edalji had been convicted in October 1903 of the mutilation of horses and cattle in Great Wyrley in Staffordshire. In

addition he was also accused of being the author of a number of threatening letters, many of which had been sent to his own home.

The case against him, which was hardly solid, began to unravel almost immediately following his conviction when the letters and mutilations continued. The police came up with all kinds of explanations for this including the notion that associates of Edalji were copying his crimes with the aim of securing his release.

Ultimately on October 19th 1906 he was released on licence[174]. This was undoubtedly due to public pressure and the media spotlight but although he was out of prison Edalji was still a convicted criminal in the eyes of the law and was thus stigmatised and barred from returning to his former profession as a solicitor.

At the time Conan Doyle was almost certainly going through a period of mixed emotions. One of these would have been loneliness. His children were away at school and Louise had been dead for a few months. The only small comfort that he had was the knowledge that it was purely a necessary and tactful delay that stood between him and marriage to Jean Leckie. It is certainly probable that he was also feeling a certain amount of guilt. Unable to do anything about Jean other than wait he was much in need of distractions.

On the day that Edalji gained his freedom Conan Doyle was enjoying one such distraction. His brother Innes had been in Amesbury, Wiltshire for an 'observation of fire course'. This had commenced on October 15th and run until the 19th. He then came to Hindhead to spend the weekend at Undershaw[175].

The following day the entry in Innes' diary is interesting:

> "Hindhead with A.C.D., Fletcher-R, Wood and Sholto Wood. 1 Round of Golf. Wrist painful."

---

[174] *Daily Express* October 20th 1906. It was essentially bail and required him to report to a police station every day.

[175] Source: The diaries of Conan Doyle and Innes Doyle for 1906.

'Fletcher-R' can only refer to Bertram Fletcher Robinson and this makes it clear, once and for all, that he and Conan Doyle were on good terms. Almost any other event involving the two men between 1901 and 1906 can be explained away but it is difficult to argue that Conan Doyle would have invited Fletcher Robinson to Hindhead for a round of golf (and for Robinson to have accepted) if the two men were not still friends.

The golf continued the following day with Innes noting in his diary that his wrist had improved and that he had beaten Conan Doyle's secretary Alfred Wood by one point. Innes was later driven to Aldershot (where he was based) in Conan Doyle's car.

November 15th saw the publication in book form of *Sir Nigel* - Conan Doyle's prequel to *The White Company*. The *Daily Express* of the same date had given it a brief review on page two. The wording of the review was interesting. The newspaper suggested that there was a view amongst many critics that the days of Conan Doyle's best work were behind him and that, in their opinion, his latest book would prove that this was not the case. They went on to say 'To these readers particularly, but also to everyone who loves a stirring, romantic story, told by a man who thoroughly realises the spirit of chivalry, and who is at the same time a born teller of tales. Sir Arthur's new story, "Sir Nigel," will be received with enthusiasm.'

This positive review is not likely to have been too much comfort to Conan Doyle who was once more alone and again in need of a diversion. The mood he was probably in made itself clear when he received a request on November 16th from The 'Times' Book Club.

The club had approached Smith, Elder and Co, who published *Sir Nigel*, and had asked to purchase nearly two thousand copies, at trade price, for their subscribers. The publishers, presumably desiring, not unreasonably, to make a profit, had refused this request. Rather than accept this, the management of the club, who were evidently determined to get copies of the book at the best possible price, decided to approach Conan Doyle. They knew that it was common practice for an author to have a contractual arrangement with their publisher whereby the author could acquire copies of their own work at the aforementioned trade price. The club requested that Conan Doyle secure the books on their behalf at this preferential rate and forward them on.

Conan Doyle was evidently disgusted by this request. However, rather than write by return to refuse, he decided to expose the club. He sent their original letter, along with his own covering letter, to *The Standard* who published both on November 20th.

Fortunately after this incident a distraction came. Once again it was courtesy of golf.

The Hindhead Golf Club had elected to hold an invitation only competition on November 26th, the principal aim of which was to beat the score of seventy-two attained by James Braid at the club's formal opening in June.

The Times of November 27th briefly covered the event. The weather conditions were sufficiently poor that Braid's score was never in any real danger of being bested. The best score at the competition's close was eighty-five with local professional S. Pownall coming in second with eighty-six. Conan Doyle distributed the prizes.

Fortunately for him, Conan Doyle's dependency on golf for distraction now came to an end as it was at around this time that Edalji's communication arrived. As a man who loathed injustice Conan Doyle would probably have taken on Edalji's case in any event but it was also just the (non-golfing) distraction he needed.

However the Christmas season brought some not unwelcome additional distractions, one of which involved Jean. On December 12th he went with Innes, his sister Dodo (Mary) and Jean to the Scala Theatre in London. According to Innes' diary they went to see '...Trevor's excellent children's plays.' Although Innes did not name the play it seems reasonable to suggest that the play in question was *Under the Greenwood Tree*. The play, which was not connected to Thomas Hardy's novel, had been mentioned only a few months earlier in *The Penny Illustrated Paper and Illustrated Times* of August 25th as 'one of the most charming children's plays imaginable'. The author, Trevor, was of course Philip Trevor who had written the piece on Conan Doyle and his rifle club a few years earlier. By this time he had risen to the rank of Major.

In the aftermath of Christmas, on December 28th, he at last focused on Edalji and discussed the case with the latest visitors to Undershaw[176]. One of these men was John Churton Collins.

Collins was Professor of English Literature at Birmingham University and was a noted literary critic. More importantly he was a student of crime and had toured the Whitechapel murder sites of Jack the Ripper with Conan Doyle and others only the previous year[177].

In 1903 Collins had co-founded 'Our Society' with H.B. Irving (the son of Henry Irving) and others. It was a society dedicated to the discussion of true crime which led to its more informal name of the Crime Club. Conan Doyle had joined the following year and in due course its ranks were added to by the likes of Bertram Fletcher Robinson and fellow novelist Max Pemberton. Its membership in 1904 totalled twelve but this grew as the society transformed from a relatively informal gathering of true crime enthusiasts into a significant organisation[178].

Over the course of the December weekend Conan Doyle talked the Edalji case through with Collins and it is almost certain that Collins' opinions influenced his approach to the case. Collins made public his personal support of Conan

---

[176] *A Chronology Of The Life of Arthur Conan Doyle* by Brian Pugh

[177] *The Life and Memoirs of John Churton Collins* by Lawrence Churton Collins.

[178] *Conan Doyle Detective* by Peter Costello.

Doyle's efforts with an article on the case in the Conservative supporting magazine *National Review*[179].

H.B. Irving co-founder of 'Our Society'

[179] According to *The Life and Memoirs of John Churton Collins* by Lawrence Churton Collins. Collins was also a fan of the Sherlock Holmes stories. He even went so far as to defend them at White's Club when they came under attack by other members. He is reported to have said 'I am indebted to Sherlock Holmes for some of the most delightful hours of my life.' According to *Conan Doyle Detective* by Peter Costello, Churton Collins may well have discussed a crime known as the Merstham Tunnel Mystery at one of the society's meetings. This crime concerned the discovery of a body of a woman who had been thrown to her death from a train. Costello puts forward the idea that this may have influenced Conan Doyle's later Holmes story *The Adventure of the Bruce-Partington Plans* which was published in *The Strand* in December 1908.

John Churton Collins (1848 - 1908)

The end of December also saw the last Christmas to be spent at Undershaw. On this occasion the guests included Lewis Waller[180].

---

[180] *Conan Doyle: The Man who Created Sherlock Holmes* by Andrew Lycett.

1907

Victory and Defeat

1907 began with further woes for the Hindhead Golf Club. Freed, by her death, of his duties to his wife, Conan Doyle had begun to take a far more active interest in the running of the club. Naturally he had listened to the opinions of his friend and secretary Alfred Wood and this had made the relationships within the club's committee even more difficult.

As club captain Whitaker was clearly feeling more and more isolated. It appears that secretary Turle and the chairman were not taking sides and this left Whitaker as the sole voice of opposition against Wood.

January brought very heavy snow to Hindhead thus effectively closing the golf course. Conan Doyle decided to take advantage of the conditions and resumed one of his other favourite pastimes - skiing.

Unfortunately he chose to do his skiing on the golf course itself which brought a rebuke from Whitaker who saw this, not unreasonably, as inappropriate.

Some momentous falling out clearly ensued between Conan Doyle, Wood and Whitaker as the captain chose to not attend any club meetings for the following eight months[181]. How the club managed to operate properly with this kind of confrontation at the top is anyone's guess.

The somewhat bad start to the year continued with the death on January 21st of Bertram Fletcher Robinson. The

---

[181] *Hindhead's Turn Will Come* by Ralph Irwin-Brown.

Daily Express, of which he had once been editor, ran a front page article in their issue of the following day.

Simply entitled *"B.F.R"*, the article stated that Robinson had died 'before he had reached the full enjoyment of his remarkable gifts' and that he had done 'more in different spheres than most men'. It went on to detail something of his experiences at Cambridge, his work as a war correspondent and his 'thrilling' detective stories. To the paper's credit its commentary on Robinson's connection to Conan Doyle and *The Hound of the Baskervilles* was little more than a line. This put things into proper context and did not permit his other work to be overshadowed. Regrettably, as time passed, his connection to Conan Doyle's famous story became, in the eyes of many, more and more important than his numerous other achievements and ultimately led to the conspiracy theories as to the story's authorship[182].

Bertram Fletcher Robinson c1902

[182] More on this can be found in *Bertram Fletcher Robinson: A Footnote to The Hound of the Baskervilles* by Brian Pugh and Paul Spiring.

The *Daily Mirror* of the same date also covered Robinson's death and stated that Conan Doyle had paid Robinson one thousand pounds for his contribution to Holmes's most famous adventure. The newspaper even went so far as to say that 'Mr. Robinson must be given the credit of inventing the plot of that famous Sherlock Holmes story...'

Conan Doyle was unable to attend Robinson's funeral in Devon and was also not able to attend the memorial service held on the 24th at St. Clement Danes Church in the Strand. The *Daily Express*, in its January 25th issue, covered the service and mentioned the presence of such literary figures as Anthony Hope and Max Pemberton but there was no mention of Conan Doyle. He was in and out of London at the time in connection with the Edalji case and therefore is likely to have been too busy despite being in the area. He visited the Home Secretary, Herbert Gladstone, in connection with Edalji on the 15th and his account of the whole affair, *The Story of Mr. George Edalji*, was published on the 20th - the day before Robinson's death.

Soon after the publication of Conan Doyle's findings, George Edalji chose to give his own account of his circumstances. The *Daily Express* of January 31st ran an article entitled *Edalij's Own Story* in which a broad outline of events was given and concluded with the fact that the account in full would be appearing in *Pearson's Weekly* from that month's issue onwards. In fact it began serialisation on February 2nd as advertisements for *Pearson's Weekly* made plain. The advertisement also, and rather helpfully, educated its readers on how to pronounce Edalji's name. A note at the bottom ran 'Most people pronounce Mr. Edalji's name wrongly. It should be pronounced Ee-dl-gee, the accent on the first E'.

The *Daily Express* of February 7th was bold enough to come out with the fact that many believed the case against Edalji to be largely based on racism. They acknowledged that he was unpopular in the neighbourhood and that his unpopularity was 'possibly deserved' but went on to say that 'it was based on the fact that by birth he is not a "white man" but half a Parsee'.

Herbert Gladstone, Home Secretary between 1905 and 1910

Towards the end of February Conan Doyle was struck down with what was then called Ptomaine poisoning. This is an outdated term today for what was effectively food poisoning caused by bacteria. Given the length of time that he was unwell it is possible that Conan Doyle was actually suffering from something akin to salmonella or listeria. It was severe enough for the *Daily Express* of March 5th to run a short article entitled *Illness of Sir A. Conan Doyle* in which he was described as 'seriously ill'.

However the newspaper was slightly behind events. *The Times* of March 8th reported that Conan Doyle had left Undershaw on both the 4th and 6th of March. The first occasion was apparently the first time he had stirred out of doors since his illness. Having determined that he was fit enough to travel Conan Doyle's second trip took him by car to Crowborough where the newspaper said he was to stay for a few days.

It is quite possible that one of his aims on the journey was to examine various properties for Jean and himself to live in. He had proposed by this time and the news was widespread within the family[183]. Of course it was neither possible nor desirable to make the news public as an official mourning period of a year was expected. The press was consequently kept in the dark until July.

April 22nd saw a recovered Conan Doyle presiding at a meeting of The Somerset Men of London at the Café Monico in Piccadilly Circus. The event had been announced publicly almost a month earlier in the letters section of the *Daily Express* of March 20th. J. Harris Stone, vice-president of the society, had announced that Conan Doyle was to chair a meeting of the society to mark the two hundredth anniversary of the birth of author Henry Fielding[184]. Stone's letter had indicated that anyone was welcome to attend regardless of whether or not they were society members.

It seems that the public at large were not overly excited by this announcement as ultimately only about one hundred and

---

[183] *Out of the Shadows* by Georgina Doyle.

[184] Fielding is most famous as the author of *Tom Jones* but also as the founder of The Bow Street Runners - the forerunner of London's police force.

fifty people attended the meeting. Conan Doyle toasted Fielding saying that no man had been truer to his ideals or had left such a mark on British literature. The toast was reportedly drunk in complete silence[185].

On Wednesday May 8th the Criterion Restaurant played host to a Society of Authors banquet. The *Daily Mirror* of the 10th covered the event and it was clear that the topics of conversation did not meet with the approval of the newspaper.

The article asked its readers what they thought would be under discussion at such a meeting. They imagined that their readership's collective response to the question would be to suppose that authors would, on such occasions, discuss writing styles and indulge in literary reminiscences. They concluded their paragraph by stating 'Not at all. The speeches were mainly about money—how to make it, and how to keep it when made'.

Singled out for special mention was George Bernard Shaw, who put it to the assembled company that the writing of plays was more profitable than novels and illustrated his argument by stating that he had once made '£6000 out of a play and only £60 for an equivalent amount of "literature in newspapers"'.

Conan Doyle, also in attendance, had taken the opportunity to land a blow against his old adversary by suggesting that Shaw keep quiet in case he had his income tax raised.

❧

The *Daily Express* of June 3rd 1907 carried an advert for a new book entitled *The Construction and Reconstruction of the Human Body*. Its author was Eugen Sandow whose bodybuilding contest Conan Doyle had attended and judged nearly six years earlier.

---

[185] *The Times* of April 23rd 1907.

Conan Doyle was so convinced of the valuable service that Sandow was performing that he agreed to write a foreword for the book. He admitted that it was the first time he had written such an introduction stating 'I have never once had the experience of getting between an author and his audience by saying a few words in advance'. He went on to state his belief that, to a large extent, physical health led to mental and spiritual health and praised Sandow by saying 'vice and ignorance are the companions of ugliness. That which is beautiful stands in the main for that which is mentally sane and spiritually sound...The man who can raise the standard of physique in any country has done something to raise all other standards as well'.

On June 7th an article appeared in the *Daily Express* concerning Edalji. The previous month had brought news of his free pardon in the pages of various newspapers yet, despite this, no official pardon had actually been executed [186]. Edalji had received no official documentation so he was forced to continue living as if he had received no pardon at all. This meant in practice that he remained a 'ticket-of-leave man' required to report constantly to the police as to his movements. The absence of official paperwork also prevented him from resuming his profession as a solicitor.

Edalji was quoted as saying 'They have deprived me of four of the most valuable years in a man's life, and I shall have to work very hard to make up for it. Yet the Home Secretary deliberately declines to send me the half a dozen lines which will allow me to start'.

People from the *Daily Express* reached Conan Doyle and he wrote a letter from the Grand Hotel which was appended to the article. Joining the newspaper's condemnation of the Home Office he concluded by saying 'The whole action of the authorities in this matter seems to me callous and heartless in the last degree quite apart from its want of justice'.

---

[186] *The Times* of May 20th was one of the newspapers.

Conan Doyle's engagement finally became public knowledge on July 9th, one year and five days since Louise Conan Doyle's death. The *Daily Express* of that date carried a one paragraph article entitled *Sir A. Conan Doyle Engaged.* Describing the groom-to-be as 'the creator of Sherlock Holmes', it confined itself to stating the month the wedding was to take place (September), the name of his fiancée and her parents and where the Leckie family resided. The story was considered important enough to make the front page but was right at the bottom sandwiched between an article on the imprisonment of the mayor of San Francisco and a breach of promise article concerning a seventy year old man.

July 22nd saw the sixth annual general meeting of Raphael Tuck & Sons. Conan Doyle had reached the end of his period as a director and was due to stand down. The meeting was chaired by Adolph Tuck and attended by a number of other Tuck family members.

Adolph and Gustave Tuck (1899)

The chairman reported that the year had been a good one despite a number of setbacks. A printing strike in Germany had forced the company to rely more heavily than usual on its British-based printing section. Despite fears that this would cause the company issues the home-based printers had successfully dealt with the increased workload.

The second significant issue was that the company had suffered from embezzlement. The chairman reported that a temporary bookkeeper, hired when the usual bookkeeper fell ill, had siphoned off money from the firm or, as they put it, 'misused the trust reposed in him.' The loss had been charged to the previous year in order to avoid it affecting the current accounts.

Conan Doyle seconded the chairman's proposal to accept the accounts. Gustave Tuck then proposed that Conan Doyle and Alfred Parsons, the two retiring directors, be re-elected. The motion was seconded and carried unopposed.

In parallel to his campaign to secure Edalji's formal pardon Conan Doyle had been working on evidence which he felt would prove the identity of the true culprit. The man he had in mind was one Royden Sharp, an apprentice butcher turned sailor with a history of forging letters at school[187]. The finished report had been sent to the Home Office a few months earlier for their consideration. However it seems that the officials there took their time before issuing a public response.

The *Daily Express* of August 13th carried the official announcement and it would not have made pleasant reading for Conan Doyle. The Home Office's official position was that Conan Doyle's report did not provide sufficient evidence for

[187] From Richard and Molly Whittington-Egan's introduction to the 1985 reissue of *The Story of Mr. George Edalji* by A. Conan Doyle.

the prosecution of Sharp (who they did not name for reasons of libel) and that no action would be taken.

On August 30th Captain Anson, the Chief Constable of Staffordshire, decided to speak to the press in response to the Home Office announcement on Conan Doyle's report and the press reaction. As the man in charge of the original case, Anson had fixed on Edalji as the culprit from early on and the entire investigation had centred on securing his conviction.

Acknowledging the criticism of his force's investigation Anson went immediately on the attack stating that 'those who complain the loudest are not always those who know the facts'. He went on to state that he was aware of Conan Doyle's report but that he had not received a copy from either the Home Office or its author and was therefore in ignorance of the man that Conan Doyle had named or 'the remarkable evidence on which this theory is based'.

In conclusion Anson stated 'all I have heard in the matter I have heard unofficially, and attach no importance to whatever. The police cannot act on theories, but must abide by facts which can be upheld beyond every shadow of doubt'.

One cannot help but marvel at the hypocrisy of Anson's criticism given that his own case would almost certainly have failed to satisfy this criterion had it been even briefly applied.

August also saw Alfred Wood chair his last meeting of the Hindhead Golf Club[188]. The fact that this was his last meeting was almost certainly down to Conan Doyle's imminent departure from the area. It was probably necessary for Wood to move too in order to be able to fulfil his role as Conan Doyle's secretary. However, even if he had wanted to stay on the club committee it is doubtful that he would have been allowed to. His presence had proved divisive and he had made an enemy

---

[188] *Hindhead's Turn Will Come* by Ralph Irwin-Brown.

in Whitaker who was no doubt glad to be seeing the back of him. Amusingly, after Wood's departure the remainder of the committee asked Whitaker if he would take over as treasurer. For reasons of his own, Whitaker refused but he did eventually become club president.

Even though the whole Wood/Conan Doyle connection had undoubtedly left a bad taste in the mouths of some club members they did gain in one important respect. The outgoing president made no attempt at the time or after his departure to call in any of his loans to the club. We can only speculate as to the reason. Perhaps he was so wrapped up in his new life that he simply forgot about the loans. Equally possible, and perhaps more likely, is that, as part of his imminent fresh start, he simply wished to draw a line under his Hindhead activities and give himself no reason for future contact

❧

The mutilations in Great Wyrley had by no means stopped during all these events. It was one of the great weaknesses of the original police case that the attacks continued even after George Edalji was in custody. The police had dealt with this problem by simply stating that the additional attacks were the work of people in league with Edalji.

The fact that Edalji was now free made no difference to the perpetrators and their latest attack was performed on Saturday August 31st and reported by the *Daily Express* the following Monday.

The latest victim was a dark brown horse belonging to a grocer by the name of Atkins. It was found by a passer-by to have an eleven inch wound along its flank.

The police, and Captain Anson, were naturally informed and a local veterinary surgeon by the coincidental name of John Watson was called on by them to examine the wound. He declared it to be caused by a sharp instrument and that it could not have been the result of an accident.

Bizarrely, the police refused to accept his findings and declared that the injury was indeed accidental. This theory was conveniently later backed up by two tannery workers who claimed to have seen the injured horse kicked by another earlier in the day.

In an effort to clarify matters, or perhaps to simply give the impression that something was being done, a reconstruction of the events leading to the discovery was made the next day. It was attended by the press, Scotland Yard and a personal representative of Conan Doyle who was not named in the resultant newspaper article. When pressed, Mr. Watson refused to retract his opinion of the wound and even signed a statement for the *Express'* reporter to restate his position. He provided perfectly logical arguments against the accident theory and the theory concerning the second horse. In his opinion the attack was the work of a copycat. The police, it appears, remained unconvinced.

Regrettably such continued nationwide coverage encouraged all manner of people to get involved. A Staffordshire farmer by the name of Snape received a postcard which ran thus:

> Beware! You are helping Conan Doyle to spoil the game. Look out for trouble Tuesday night.

The poor farmer was compelled to fortify his farm and stay up during the night with a gun just in case[189]. Another postcard arrived for Atkins, the owner of the earlier mutilated horse and the veterinarian John Watson received a communication that supposedly explained how the earlier crime was performed. No details were reported other than Mr. Watson had handed the letter to the police.

From much of the newspaper coverage at the time you would be forgiven for getting the impression that the pubic and press were very much united against what was presented as the

---

[189] *Daily Express* September 4th 1907.

incompetence of the Staffordshire police. This, although largely true, was certainly not completely so. On September 14th the editor of *The Penny Illustrated Paper and Illustrated Times* decided to come to the defence of the police. In the section *The Editor to his Friends* he remarked on the number of letters received at his newspaper and others from people who knew 'exactly how the police may lay their hands on the perpetrators of the crime'. He was disdainful of many of these people and maintained that the average policeman 'could do more detecting in five minutes than all these theorists could accomplish in a lifetime'. He also professed to be at a loss as to why so many people were convinced that Conan Doyle would be able to succeed where the police had failed.

> 'With all due respect to a very clever man, I quite fail to see why Sir Arthur should succeed where the police have been at fault. Bear in mind that there is nothing easier, to a man who makes his living that way, than to invent a crime and then find the perpetrator of it'.

He concluded by telling his readers that the police succeeded more often than they failed and that if his readers considered the life of an ordinary policeman to be 'very prosaic' they should consider how little they would like to try 'waking up a good-sized drunken navvy and telling him that you are going to arrest him'.

Conan Doyle may well have been hoping for a few peaceful days in the lead up to his wedding. It appears however that he indulged himself in a few social engagements. On September 12th he went to the Drury Lane Theatre, to see the play *The Sins of Society*, as a guest of Mrs Arthur Collins - the wife of the theatre's manager[190]. While the party watched the play, Mrs

[190] The event was reported in the *Daily Express* of the following day.

Collins' jewellery box, the contents of which were reported to be worth £500, was stolen from an adjoining room where it had been placed by her maid. All attempts at locating the missing jewellery failed and the theft was reported to the police. Strangely the press coverage managed to avoid mentioning Sherlock Holmes even though Conan Doyle's name was prominent in the reports.

September 17th saw Conan Doyle's wedding-eve party which was held at the Gaiety Restaurant. The restaurant was based very close to the theatre of the same name and this reflected the fact that when the theatre had first been founded the restaurant was part of the business.

The diary of Innes Doyle stated that he arrived at the Grand Hotel at approximately 6pm[191]. Although it is not stated one presumes that Conan Doyle himself was also at the hotel and had probably arranged his brother's room. Innes went on to list those attending the meal. Assuming his list to be complete it seems it was a relatively small affair. Aside from Conan Doyle and Innes those attending included John and Archie Langman, Alfred Wood, Major Guggisberg, Captain Trevor, Cyril Angell, Willie Hornung, and A.C.R. Williams.

---

[191] Courtesy of Georgina Doyle.

The Gaiety Theatre in 1912. The restaurant was close by.
(Author's collection)

Farewell Undershaw

September 18th brought the marriage of Conan Doyle to Jean Leckie. In order to control the amount of press attention, Conan Doyle kept the exact location a secret. The *Daily Express* of that day confirmed this in a short article on their front page under the heading *Today's Story*.

The same paper expanded on the story on page five under the heading *Novelist's Wedding*. It would appear that, in order to placate the press, Conan Doyle gave certain details of the event to them perhaps in the hope that they would be considerate of his privacy.

The article repeated that the wedding was to take place at a secret location with 'only a few relatives and friends' present. The bride's dress was described as being of 'silver tissue veiled with silk lace and embroidered in pearls'. Aside from similar descriptions of the bridesmaids' outfits the article stated that the majority of guests would only attend the reception and that afterwards the newlyweds 'will spend their honeymoon on the Continent'.

The following day the press reported in earnest. The *Daily Express* gave a detailed account right down to the chosen music. Given that the press was not invited we must assume that the information was again provided to them by the family.

However, the event did not entirely elude the press despite Conan Doyle's best efforts. Page nine of the same newspaper carried a picture of Conan Doyle and his new bride leaving the church. Part of the caption clearly indicated that someone not on the guest list had obtained it. It stated 'Sir Arthur would not reveal the name of the church at which the ceremony was to take place. He forgot, however, that Sherlock Holmes educated the public in solving mysteries like this for themselves'[192].

Whether this meant that the press had figured out the location and had lain in wait or that some passer-by had obtained the photograph and sold it to the press is not clear.

The New York Times of the same date gave details, again presumably supplied by the family, of the bride and groom's presents to each other. Jean presented Conan Doyle with a gold watch and he gave her a 'superb' diamond tiara. The article also suggested how the wedding may have come to be photographed. Mention was made of spectators that had gathered outside the church due to the unexpected ringing of its bells and 'the awning before the entrance.' The newspaper then concluded its article with the statement 'Sir Conan had long been regarded as a confirmed bachelor. He is 48 years old.' Aside from the odd use of his name it was a bizarre statement as Conan Doyle had only been a widower for just over fourteen months and most of this time had been the expected mourning period.

The reception took place at the Hotel Metropole on Northumberland Avenue. Conan Doyle and Jean arrived earlier than they were supposed to and before anyone was ready to receive them. The amusing result of this was that Conan Doyle had to act as his wife's trainbearer up the steps into the hotel[193].

Inside some three hundred guests had assembled. According to the reports, the first of these to offer his congratulations was George Edalji. Edalji's presents to the couple were complete volumes of Shakespeare and Tennyson.

---

[192] In his diary for September 18th Innes Doyle remarks that the wedding was 'Almost private'. It seems quite likely that this remark referred to members of the public who were outside the church and may have included the person taking the photograph which later appeared in the press.

[193] *Daily Express* September 19th 1907.

The remainder of the guest list read like a who's who of writing and publishing. Names included Bram Stoker, J.M. Barrie, Jerome K. Jerome, Max Pemberton, George Newnes and Herbert Greenhough Smith.

Although it was almost certainly not uppermost in his mind, Conan Doyle needed to decide what to do with Undershaw. His new wife clearly did not want to live in the house of her predecessor and presumably wanted to remain close to her family. Because of this Conan Doyle had clearly hunted for suitable properties in Crowborough in the intervening months before the wedding. The two obvious options for Undershaw were to either sell it or lease it. Conan Doyle elected to do the latter and it seems likely, given his departure on honeymoon, that this task was delegated to Alfred Wood. The *Daily Express* of October 9th remarked that 'Sir Arthur Conan Doyle has disposed of his house at Haslemere, and on the return from their honeymoon he and Lady Doyle will take up their residence at Windlesham, Crowborough'.

The suggestion was that a new occupier had been found but his identity was not revealed until December when *The Times* of December 25th revealed that the new occupier of Undershaw would be Canon Edward Carus Selwyn, the retiring headmaster of Uppingham School.

Why did Conan Doyle retain Undershaw? With this question we enter firmly into the realm of speculation. It is possible that in the short-term he kept it purely as an additional source of income. Perhaps he also did so with a view to giving it to Kingsley when he came of age.[194] As the location of Louise Conan Doyle's final years and death it would no doubt have held many important memories for both of her children.

---

[194] Conan Doyle retained ownership of Undershaw until 1921 when he finally put it up for sale. By this time he was clearly eager to be rid of it as the article in *The Times* of May 10th 1921 stated that 'a very low price' would be accepted in order to ensure 'an immediate sale'.

ꕥ

The wedding drew the line under Conan Doyle's connection not only with Undershaw but with Hindhead. Regrettably this same period also saw the beginning of the apparently negative impact of Jean's presence as step-mother on the lives of Conan Doyle's children. It comes across, from the information available, as though Jean wanted to pretend that Conan Doyle's earlier marriage and children never happened. Despite her wish to be with the family for Christmas, Mary Conan Doyle was forced to stay in Germany where she was studying and her brother Kingsley stayed with the Hornungs.

Conan Doyle's complicity in this does not reflect well on him. For him the outlook was good. He had a new wife, a promising future and was no longer having to tip-toe with Jean through polite society. For his children the situation was very much at the other end of the spectrum and it was a time when they really needed their father. Their mother had only been dead eighteen months and this was only their second Christmas without her. To be forced to spend it without their blissfully happy father as well was the height of cruelty.

However for Conan Doyle his life was, once again, an entirely new country.

Entering the 21st Century

Undershaw Today

Hopefully I have made it clear within these pages that a lot of importance happened in the life of Arthur Conan Doyle during the time that Hindhead and Undershaw were his home. It was for this reason that I played (and am still playing) a small part in the efforts to preserve it.

Below are a selection of photographs of the building taken around 2007 which illustrate the condition the house is now in. Please note that the British system of floor numbering is used.

Conan Doyle outside Undershaw's front door
(Courtesy of Georgina Doyle)

The view from inside looking towards the same door today (Courtesy of The Undershaw Preservation Trust)

The Drawing Room where Conan Doyle entertained people such as Bram Stoker
(Courtesy of The Undershaw Preservation Trust)

The billiard room
(Courtesy of The Undershaw Preservation Trust)

Louise's bedroom on the first floor where she almost certainly died in 1906
(Courtesy of The Undershaw Preservation Trust)

The first floor nursery where Mary and Kingsley would have played (Courtesy of The Undershaw Preservation Trust)

2nd floor corridor leading towards the servants' rooms
(Courtesy of The Undershaw Preservation Trust)

The servants' stairs from the kitchen upwards
(Courtesy of The Undershaw Preservation Trust)

Bibliography

Carr, John Dickson - *The Life of Sir Arthur Conan Doyle*. Avalon Publishing Group. ISBN-13: 978-0786712342.

Collins, Lawrence Churton - *The Life and Memoirs of John Churton Collins*. Kessinger Publishing (3 Nov 2007). ISBN-13: 978-0548695333.

Costello, Peter - *Conan Doyle Detective*. Caroll & Graff (2006). ISBN13 978-0-78671-855-9.

Doyle, Arthur Conan - *Memories and Adventures*. Wordsworth Editions Ltd. ISBN-13: 978-1840225709.

Doyle, Arthur Conan - *The Story of Mr. George Edalji*. Camille Wolff Grey House Books; New edition (Jun 1985). 978-0951060407.

Doyle, Arthur Conan - *Through the Magic Door*.

Doyle, Georgina - *Out of the Shadows*. Ash Tree Pr (30 Jun 2004). ISBN-13: 978-1553100645.

Duncan, Alistair - *Close to Holmes*. MX Publishing (1 Feb 2009). ISBN-13: 978-1904312505.

Duncan, Alistair - *The Norwood Author.* MX Publishing (1 Mar 2010). ISBN-13: 978-1904312697.

Gibson, John; Green, Richard Lancelyn - *A Bibliography of A. Conan Doyle*. Hudson House. ISBN-13: 978-0967750002.

Gibson, John; Green, Richard Lancelyn - *Letters to the Press.* Martin Secker & Warburg Ltd (19 Feb 1986). ISBN-13: 978-0436133039.

Higham, Charles - *The Adventures of Conan Doyle*. Hamish Hamilton 1976. SBN 241 89498 0.

Irwin-Brown, Ralph - *Hindhead's Turn Will Come*. Self-published. ISBN-13: 978-0951773000.

Lellenberg Jon, Stashower, Daniel, Foley Charles - *Arthur Conan Doyle: A Life in Letters*. Harper Press (17 Sep 2007). ISBN-13: 978-0007247592

Lycett, Andrew - *Conan Doyle: The Man who created Sherlock Holmes*. Weidenfeld & Nicolson; First Edition (30 Aug 2007).ISBN-13: 978-0297848523

Malec, Andrew - *Molding the Image: William Gillette as Sherlock Holmes*. Special Collections O. Meredith Wilson Library University of Minnesota (1983)

O'Donovan, John - *Shaw and the Charlatan Genius*. Dolmen Press (Sep 1965). ISBN-13: 978-0851050911.

Pearce, Brian - *Cricket at the Crystal Palace*. Crystal Palace Foundation (8 Sep 2004). ISBN-13: 978-1897754092.

Pugh, Brian - *A Chronology of the Life of Arthur Conan Doyle*. MX Publishing; 1st edition (22 May 2009). ISBN-13: 978-1904312550.

Sandow, Eugen - *The Construction and Reconstruction of the Human Body.* John Bale, Sons and Danielsson Limited (1907).

Spiring, Paul - *A Bibliography of Bertram Fletcher Robinson.* Privately published.

Stoker, Bram. *Personal Reminiscences of Henry Irving Volume II.* William Heinemann 1906.

Tracy, Jack. *Sherlock Holmes - The Published Apocrypha.* Gaslight Publications. ISBN 0-93-446824-9.

Whitt, J.F. - *The Strand Magazine 1891 - 1950 A Selective Checklist.* Privately published ISBN: 0 9506700 0 6.

Zecher, Henry - *William Gillette: America's Sherlock Holmes.* Xlibris Corporation (26 Mar 2011). ISBN-13: 978-1453555804.

Index

Also from MX Publishing

Close To Holmes

A Look at the Connections Between Historical London, Sherlock Holmes and Sir Arthur Conan Doyle.

Eliminate The Impossible

An Examination of the World of Sherlock Holmes on Page and Screen.

The Norwood Author

Arthur Conan Doyle and the Norwood Years (1891 - 1894). Winner of the 2011 Howlett Literary Award – Sherlock Holmes book of the year.

Also From MX Publishing

In Search of Dr Watson

Wonderful biography of Dr.Watson from expert Molly Carr. Now fully updated 2nd edition.

Arthur Conan Doyle, Sherlock Holmes and Devon

A Complete Tour Guide and Companion. Nominated for the 2011 Howlett Literary Award.

The Lost Stories of Sherlock Holmes

Eight more stories from the pen of John H Watson – compiled by Tony Reynolds.

Also From MX Publishing

Watsons Afghan Adventure

Fascinating biography of Watson's time in Afghanistan from US Army veteran Kieran McMullen.

Shadowfall

Sherlock Holmes, ancient relics and demons and mystic characters. A supernatural Holmes pastiche.

Official Papers of The Hound of The Baskervilles

Very unusual collection of the original police papers from The Hound case.

Also From MX Publishing

The Sign of Fear

The first adventure of the 'female Sherlock Holmes'. A delightful fun adventure with your favourite supporting Holmes characters.

A Study in Crimson

The second adventure of the 'female Sherlock Holmes' with a host of sub-plots and new characters joining Watson and Fanshaw

The Chronology of Arthur Conan Doyle

The definitive chronology used by historians and libraries worldwide.

Also From MX Publishing

Aside Arthur Conan Doyle

A collection of twenty stories from ACD's close friend Bertram Fletcher Robinson.

Bertram Fletcher Robinson

The comprehensive biography of the assistant plot producer of The Hound of The Baskervilles

Wheels of Anarchy

Reprint and introduction to Max Pemberton's thriller from 100 years ago. One of the first spy thrillers of its kind.

Also From MX Publishing

Bobbles and Plum

Four playlets from PG Wodehouse 'lost' for over 100 years – found and reprinted with an excellent commentary

The World of Vanity Fair

A specialist full-colour reproduction of key articles from Bertram Fletcher Robinson containing of colour caricatures from the early 1900s.

Tras Las He huellas de Arthur Conan Doyle (in Spanish)

Un viaje ilustrado por Devon.

Also From MX Publishing

The Case of The Grave Accusation

The creator of Sherlock Holmes has been accused of murder. Only Holmes and Watson can stop the destruction of the Holmes legacy.

Barefoot on Baker Street

Epic novel of the life of a Victorian workhouse orphan featuring Sherlock Holmes and Moriarty.

Case of Witchcraft

A tale of witchcraft in the Northern Isles, in which some long-concealed secrets are revealed including about the Great Detective himself.

Also From MX Publishing

The Case of The Russian Chessboard

Short novel covering the dark world of Russian espionage sees Holmes and Watson on the world stage facing dark and complex enemies.

Lightning Source UK Ltd.
Milton Keynes UK
UKOW031920210512

192990UK00002B/4/P